one

STELLA LET OUT A DEEP, relaxed sigh as her muscles softened into the plush lounge chair. The setting sun cast a warm glow on her face, and the steady sound of waves filled the air. Even with the slight breeze, she was comfortable and slightly buzzed from the rum. She couldn't help but smile.

It was simple yet perfect. This was her own little slice of paradise.

A splash interrupted the quiet, and soon enough, a hand landed gently on her ankle. His rough fingers traced a teasing path over her skin, igniting a trail of shivers that danced up her leg. He chuckled softly at her side, grazing the goosebumps around her knee. She tried to hold back a smirk, but he caught it.

"Not disturbing you, am I?"

"Uh-uh. Nothing could possibly disturb me here."

Taking the challenge, he adjusted his grip, his strong fingers lightly skimming her thigh with a deliberate slowness that drew her closer. The blue fabric of her swimsuit sat snugly on her hips, curving up and around her ass, showing just a hint of pale skin beneath. He traced a finger along the line of flimsy material before quickly skipping up to her stomach, which was still wet from her swim.

Then, all at once, his hand was gone, and though she didn't feel him move, his shadow blocked the sun, leaving her cold. She felt her nipples harden and opened her eyes, raising a disapproving brow his way.

"You mind?"

"I just needed a better view," he replied, his dark eyes drinking in every inch of her tanned body. "But something isn't quite right."

Stella frowned, confused for a few seconds before the penny dropped. Shaking her head, she lifted her hands to the skinny straps holding her bikini top in place. With her eyes locked on his, she tucked her thumbs under the blue elastic and gave each one the slightest tug. They fell off her shoulders, but the damp bikini stayed put.

"I guess I could lose the top, huh?"

She brushed a finger across her right breast and squinted up at him. He shrugged, giving her an innocent look that said, 'Oh, I don't know.' But his eyes were intense and needy, watching intently as she shifted on the sun bed. They widened when she sat up and freed her breasts with a single tug. But with the top still tied at the back, they held in place. Perky, bouncy, and practically served up on a platter.

And he didn't need an invitation. Instead, he pounced, his knees hitting the sand at the same time his fingertips found her nipples.

Stella gasped when his mouth touched her. Her clit pulsed as his tongue swirled. She closed her eyes, happy to let him play, knowing full well he'd need to go lower soon enough.

As if reading her mind, his right hand left her breast, and she tensed, knowing exactly where it was going. Her stomach rippled at his touch until he reached her covered mound. She shuddered, his fingers stroking slowly and carefully. Then, finding her slit, he added just enough pressure to draw a sharp gasp.

When they finally flicked under the side of the bikini, Stella held her breath. His teeth tugged at her nipple, clamping down

remodeling romance

elizabeth hardy

right as his fingers reached her sex. She was wet and aching for him, but didn't want this to end.

Skillfully, he worked her opening, running his hands around and around until, finally, he moved up to her most sensitive spot. The pressure on her nipples increased when he touched her, causing her back to arch and a moan to rush from her mouth.

He responded with a kiss, capturing her pleasure with his lips and tongue. At the same time, he rubbed her clit until he could feel she was close. But his hand came away too soon.

Standing quickly, he reached with both hands to remove her bikini bottoms before shifting to his own waist. Stella couldn't help but lick her lips when his rock-hard cock popped free. She reached for it eagerly, and he stepped just close enough for the tip to meet her tongue. Stella smiled and opened wide, letting him inside. A warm, salty-sweet taste filled her mouth, and she lifted her eyes to his, licking and sucking until he bit his lip.

Finding his balls with one hand, she took hold of his length with the other. She squeezed and stroked in tandem with her mouth, pleasuring as much of him as she could at once.

"Fuuuuck." He groaned.

She could feel him throbbing against her tongue and wondered if he would last long enough to fuck her.

She should've known better.

He laced his fingers into her hair and tugged her head back. In one swift motion, he reached behind and adjusted the sunbed to make it flat. Then he was on her, his knees shifting her legs apart and his tongue bursting into her mouth.

He entered her hard and fast, both of them letting out a moan of pleasure when he was all the way in. Stella's breath caught as his lips returned to her nipple. Between that and the feeling of his length inside, she could already feel the pressure building.

Picking up the pace, he lifted his torso and grabbed hold of her thighs for support. He pounded into her a dozen times before taking a breath and slowing. Then he licked his fingers and found her clit once more.

They slipped into place like they were made for her, gliding in time with his thick cock. Stella reached up and put a hand on his chest. Her eyes found his, and she felt her stomach contract.

Dark Eyes, don't fail me now.

She yanked him down and kissed him until she couldn't catch her breath. His torture of her clit was relentless, and she felt her legs begin to twitch. Her orgasm was racing head-on, and just when she thought she'd explode—

"What the fuck, bro? Didn't you see me?"

Stella's eyes shot open, and she released a staggered, frustrated breath.

"No. No! I'm the leader on this, so you do what the fuck I say."

You've got to be fucking kidding me.

For a brief moment, she tried to go on. She pressed the vibe to her clit and rubbed, eyes squeezed shut as she tugged at her nipple. But it was no use. It was gone.

Pulling the little bullet free, she clicked it off, and the sudden lack of humming made the room feel deathly quiet. Apart from Todd, of course. He was busy screaming into a headset over a dumb video game.

I was this *close!*

Stella fell back into the bed and ran a hand over her forehead. It had been weeks since she'd last climaxed, alone or with Todd, and it was starting to get to her. For whatever reason, she just couldn't get there.

So, that night, she'd given herself time to set the mood. Todd had a new game that would keep him busy for hours, leaving her to a quiet bedroom and some alone time. She had a couple of cocktails and read a steamy novel. Then, she sat herself down and let her imagination run wild.

Picturing the gorgeous construction guy she had a major crush on, Stella took her time, toying with her nipples as the beach fantasy played out.

She imagined his big arms wrapped around her. His tight ass

in those jeans he always wore. And the way he smiled at her—or at least, the way she thought he smiled at her.

By the time she reached for the bullet, she was wet and ready. And the guy was there to please her. She'd all but felt his lips on her skin and was seconds from release when fucking Todd decided he couldn't use his inside voice.

It took a few calming breaths before she even thought about getting out of bed. Then, she methodically cleaned the toy, put it away, and took the time to shower. She washed away the lube, letting the hot water run over her newly pounding head.

When she was done, she'd calmed enough to face him. Although, more and more, she found she didn't really want to.

two

. . .

WITH HER HAND on the doorknob, Stella felt her blood boiling. She heard him down the hall, screaming into his headset, complaining to his 'team' about their poor performance.

Talk about irony.

After a few more deep breaths, she managed to plaster on a smile and opened the door. But she immediately wished she hadn't bothered. She barely took two steps out of their room before she hit a box full to the brim with his crap. The same box she'd asked him to move days ago.

And two steps beyond that was a new box—and then another.

They weren't moving into the new place for another few months, but their lease was up in a week. So, packing had commenced, and she'd booked an Airbnb until the house was ready. Stella was mostly done, having left out a few basics for the remaining days.

Todd's stuff, on the other hand, was all over.

When she reached the living room, her heart sank further. He was sitting on the white sofa, perched on the end with a bag of chips at his side and multiple cans of Red Bull on the table. An empty bag of fast food sat at his feet, and the smell of stale fries filled the room.

On the TV—the too-big monstrosity Todd insisted they needed —characters ran around and shot at zombies or soldiers or something equally as juvenile. The way they talked, you'd think they were real soldiers. Discussing tactics and strategy as if they were under siege.

In reality, they were nothing more than sad, lonely morons, with nothing better to do with their lives.

Standing in the hallway, she sighed, not wanting to get too close. "Babe?"

He responded by blowing something up.

"Did you see that? Did you fucking see that? Bro! You gotta get the—"

"Todd?" Stella called out. "Hello?"

"Oh, uh, hey, babe. What's up?" he asked without turning to face her.

"Could you maybe keep it down? I mean, it's pretty late. We've talked about this and—"

"Fuck you, Tom. You pussy!"

"Todd?"

He sighed and mumbled into his microphone. The screen froze, and he made a show of turning around, eyebrows raised like a frustrated teenager.

"What is it?"

"You can't be screaming into that thing so late. The neighbors are gonna complain."

He laughed and shrugged. "We're moving. Who gives a shit?"

"I do. I give a shit. I like our neighbors and—"

"Okay, okay," he cooed, raising his hands in surrender.

When he moved to stand, Stella tensed. He stepped over the crap on the floor and sauntered her way, a swing in his step and his eyes low.

"I figured you'd be more relaxed after your little…you know. Bzzzzz sesh." He took her hand and smirked. "Let me guess," he began, circling his arms around her waist. "You need the real thing."

His lips were on her neck before she could answer. He smelled like Red Bull, and she could tell he hadn't showered in at least a day.

"No, babe. Your game—"

Todd put a salty finger on her lips and shushed her. "Fuck 'em."

She wanted to stop it, to tell him not to bother. But he could be such a baby when he didn't get his way. So, it was easier to let him do his thing. It didn't last long these days, anyway.

His cold hands slipped under her shirt and found her tits in seconds. He roughly grabbed at her and pushed her back—the way confident men did in the movies. With Todd, though, it just felt awkward. They stumbled into the bedroom, and he crashed down on top of her. His tongue was sloppy and rough when they kissed, and their teeth clashed every time Stella shifted under his weight.

Not a minute went by before his hand was down her sweatpants. His fingers rubbed over her still-wet slit, chafing and causing her to wince.

"Wait, babe. I'm not…there." Stella grabbed his hand.

Todd laughed. "Oh, I get it."

The next thing she knew, he was between her legs, his quick tongue somehow managing to miss her clit with every pass. She didn't know when he'd gotten so bad at this, but she couldn't help but feel responsible. She'd faked it so many times to keep him from feeling bad that he didn't do anything to change his technique.

Reaching to the bedside, Stella grabbed the lube. "Here, babe. I want you inside."

She tried to make her tone sexy, and he seemed to buy it. He slathered the warming lube over his dick and between her legs, brushing past her clit a few times by mistake. Then he was inside, thrusting and grunting over her like a horny teen.

Stella closed her eyes and pictured the sexy construction guy. *Dark Eyes.*

She thought about the time she'd caught him watching her and how his big arms glistened in the sun. She tried to get back to the beach, where she was warm, wet, and happy.

Slipping her hand between them, Stella found her mound and circled it. She imagined Dark Eyes' hands on her, big, strong, and dominating. Maybe he liked kink and would spank her? Or maybe he wanted to take her from behind, one hand in her hair as he rammed inside?

As if by magic, Stella felt the pressure building. And finally, with her eyes closed and her mind in her fantasy, she actually felt like she might climax. She picked up the pace, using more pressure as she desperately tried to cum before Todd. When she heard him groan, she ignored it. Even as he finished, shuddering beside her, she kept going.

His hands are on my ass, and he's spanking me. He's holding my wrists down as he sucks my nipples. His big rough fingers are on my clit, and he's rubbing and rubbing and—

"Oh!" Stella felt a rush as a small orgasm hit. It was short-lived, but she felt a wave of relief. So much so, it brought a tear to her eye.

Todd was already rolling away, catching his breath at her side.

"You're welcome." He smirked before getting up and padding naked to the living room.

She heard the game start up again as he joked about needing to please his woman.

Stella rolled onto her side and used his pillow to wipe her eyes. She got up and took another shower. On her way back to the bed, she glanced at the clock and smiled, wondering how many of the little idiots in his headset had taken note of the whole eight minutes Todd was gone.

three

· · ·

"DAMN, babe. You don't look so good."

Stella rolled her eyes as the guy behind the counter scribbled her name on a cup and handed it off to the barista.

"Thanks." She quickly stepped aside to let Jenny order and scanned the crowded café for a free table.

"You okay?" Jenny asked, eyes on her phone.

"Just tired."

Stella's gaze drifted out the window as she wished for the hundredth time that her meeting wasn't scheduled so early. Suppressing a yawn, she craned her neck to see if a couple near the door were gathering their belongings. No luck.

"Let me guess," Jenny started, tossing the phone into her purse. "That shithead kept you up all night gaming?"

"How'd you know?" The sarcasm in her tone was thick.

Before Jenny could respond, the young girl behind the espresso machine called out Stella's name. She stepped forward and smiled her thanks, taking a quick sip with her eyes closed.

I'm gonna need more than this to get through today.

She tuned out a loud customer nearby and focused on the coffee, mentally reviewing the upcoming meeting's key points. By the time Jenny joined her with her own drink, Stella spotted a couple vacating a spot by the back wall. She quickly claimed the table, snagging a chair before a gaggle of yoga moms could reach it.

"Stells, it's time to cut the fucking cord. I mean, seriously. How long are you gonna pretend this moron makes you happy?"

"Jen, I—"

"No, babe. Don't try that shit with me. I know you. I can see you're not happy."

Stella shrugged. She didn't have the energy for this again. "Jenny, come on. He stayed with me when—"

"*When your sister died*, I know. Even I can admit he was great back then. But that was two years ago, and he only did what any decent human would do. It doesn't give him a pass to mooch off you and be an asshole now."

In the beginning, Stella and Todd were hot and heavy. They'd met at a bar through a mutual friend and immediately hit it off. He was sweet, funny, and spontaneous. He listened to her and brought her coffee when she was having a bad day. He ran to the store for tampons when she was out, and he even did her laundry when his roommate's cat peed on her jeans.

But then her sister died suddenly, and she'd been a wreck. Being the younger of the two, Stella had always idolized Cynthia. So, between the shock and the grief, it was all she could do to get up in the morning.

Her relationship with Todd was still new then, just a few months old. In truth, she'd expected him to run for the hills. But he didn't. Instead, he basically moved in. He held her as she cried herself to sleep and was there to help with everything from the funeral arrangements to finding her parents a decent therapist.

Todd had been her rock, and she knew she wouldn't have gotten through it all without him. But a year later, he lost his job, and he'd been floating ever since.

Gaming was the new thing. He'd planned to stream full-time, which would, in his words, "be more than enough to pay the bills." But after six months, all he had was a dozen or so subscribers and a ton of debt.

And then there was the sex.

Thinking back, it had never been great—or even very good. But Todd was nice and funny, so Stella gave him a chance. And it wasn't horrific. He was just a little too quick to get things going and wasn't the best multitasker in the world. He couldn't thrust and use his hands at the same time. Shit, he couldn't even lick and use his fingers together.

Then, after the dust settled with her sister, Stella just assumed it was her fault. *She* wasn't enough. *She* wasn't right. *She* needed fixing.

Yet the longer it went on, the more the truth became clear. *He* wasn't attentive. *He* didn't take direction or criticism well. And *he* wasn't interested in foreplay.

Of course, it didn't help that the longer he remained unemployed, the less she found herself attracted to him. Not that his job had been a big draw for her. He just stopped trying. He stopped getting dressed in the mornings and stopped taking care of himself. Instead, he spent hours in front of the TV, watching dumb YouTube videos and insisting he should start a channel of his own.

At first, she assumed he'd find a new job and get back to work —and to his old self—pretty fast. Todd was a copywriter, and though it could be boring sometimes, it paid surprisingly well. Hell, she was even on board with him working from home. Plenty of jobs offered remote opportunities so Todd could ease back into things from the comfort of their couch. But he wasn't interested.

The guilt made her stay. She knew that losing his job had been a big blow, and if she left him because of it, what would that make her? After everything he'd done when she'd needed him the most?

Not that Jenny cared. All she saw was the freeloader who made her best friend miserable.

"Can we talk about something else?" Stella asked, a tired smile on her face.

Jenny furrowed her brow and pursed her lips but nodded. "Fine. How's the house?"

That was enough to perk her up. Stella bit her lip and quietly clapped her hands with glee. "It looks amazing. Seriously, I can't wait to move in. We're going to see it later and speak with the contractor about tiles for the kitchen and bathrooms."

"Wow, that's great. Last time I was there, it was a mess."

"Oh, come on. It wasn't a mess—it was a construction site. And the guys had barely started."

"Speaking of construction guys…" Jenny took a bite of her bagel and raised her eyebrows suggestively.

With a slight shrug, Stella chose her words carefully. "You need to stop with that shit. It's like sexual harassment or something. I'm his boss, remember?"

Since day one, she'd had a crush on Dark Eyes and stupidly told Jenny all about it. Though she kept her sexual fantasies to herself.

"Oh, please. He'd love it. The big boss lady strolling in and demanding he please her. If he's anything like I'm picturing, I bet he's got huge hands and a dick for days."

Stella chuckled into her coffee. The older woman on her left was less amused.

"I don't even know his name. And yeah, he's working for me now, but in a few weeks, he'll be gone. On to torture the next desperate housewife with his dark eyes and perfect jaw."

"So you have been looking!"

They both laughed, and Stella blushed. She'd done a lot of looking since the day he walked onto the job site. All six feet of him. More than once, she'd found herself staring from the car as he moved in and out of the house, something big and heavy nestled on his toned shoulders.

"It doesn't matter," she muttered. "He's off limits."

———

After breakfast, Stella rushed to the office to meet a new client. As the lead accountant at her firm, they needed her to explain exactly why the new money multi-millionaire couldn't buy the Dodgers. It took a bit of convincing, but he finally settled on investing—and a beachfront property in Belize.

Lunch rolled around, and her excitement grew. She hadn't been to the house in a couple of weeks, but she'd seen pictures of the progress. Almost all the walls were up, and they were working on the upstairs framing. The kitchen and bathroom tiles were the next big thing.

Grabbing her phone, she sent a quick text to remind Todd to be ready at noon.

> Hey. I'll leave the office in around 30. Meet me outside, ok?

He didn't reply. She tried him again, texting twice more before calling on her way to the car. When he didn't answer, Stella felt her pulse quicken and her neck flush with anger. She bit her cheek and mentally prepared herself for another fight.

In front of the apartment, Todd was nowhere in sight. Not bothering to call him again, she left the car at the curb and ran upstairs. Storming inside, she found him passed out on the bed, fully clothed, with another can of Red Bull on the side table.

"Todd? What the fuck?"

He didn't even stir when she yelled his name again and slammed the door. It took moving around the bed and shaking his shoulder to get a grunt.

"Todd. Seriously? We have to be at the house! You know I don't have long."

"Huh?" He groaned, his breath a disgusting mix of sweet energy drink and mid-morning breath. "What? Oh, shit. Sorry, babe. I, uh—"

"Just get dressed, for fuck's sake."

Back in the living room, Stella had a sudden urge to grab his shit and toss it at the still-on TV. Luckily, she resisted and made it back to the car without breaking anything. Todd joined her five minutes later, looking like shit and smelling like a frat house.

"Stell—"

"Don't." She kept her eyes on the road and gritted her teeth. And for once, Todd stayed quiet.

four

. . .

AS ANGRY AS SHE WAS, the minute Stella pulled onto her street, the tension melted away. Her new house sat on the right, still under construction but looking bigger and better than ever.

She'd been saving for almost a decade, and thanks to an appreciative client who just happened to be an architect, she managed to afford something spectacular.

"What the hell is with the porch?" Todd asked, sticking his head forward and ruining her moment. "I thought we agreed on columns?"

We didn't agree on shit.

Confused, he looked at her with his mouth agape, but she kept her eyes on the road. Since it was all her money paying for it, she had the final say. And she definitely didn't want tacky columns.

"I told you I want a porch big enough to fit a swing." Stella rolled her eyes and pulled up just beyond the house and behind the contractor's car.

The warm wind whipped her hair as she stepped out and covered her eyes to get a better look at the front. The windows weren't in yet, and they'd hung a temporary front door, but they'd made a lot of progress. Excitedly, she hurried forward and up the steps, forgetting all about Todd in her wake.

A couple of guys were working on the corner, and they smiled and nodded when they saw her. She'd been bringing them donuts and beers every now and then to keep them happy, and it seemed to be working. They were quick and efficient. The house was on schedule and looked better than she'd imagined.

"Marco?" Stella called out when she walked inside, her eyes widening with joy.

The stairway was almost finished. It ran up the side wall to the top level, which was open and full of light. The structural walls for the office and bathroom were in place on the right, and she could see the skeleton of a kitchen to the left.

"Stella! Nice to see you." Marco smiled, taking her hand in his and pulling her into the middle of the big room. "What do you think?" He waved his arm at the stairs and winked.

"It looks…" She scanned the room and covered her mouth in delight. Only one word came to mind. "Perfect. It's perfect, Marco. Thank you."

"Well, I know how much you wanted the—"

"Boss? You got the frames for that back door coming sometime today?"

They both turned to see one of the workers rushing their way. Marco put his hands together and apologized to Stella for the interruption. Then he turned and raised his voice just loud enough for the other men in the room to get the gist: the client's here, so shut the fuck up.

"I told you it would be here after lunch. Is it after lunch yet?"

"No, but they need the frame in so they can get the floor going. Since she wanted—"

"Miss Young asked for the seamless entry into the mud room, yes. And you can get to it as soon as the frame arrives."

Stella could see he was smiling, but it was more like a grimace. The worker nodded and hustled away, his tail between his legs. She watched him, feeling bad that he'd gotten in trouble—until he reached the doorway. A second later, another man appeared.

The man. Mr. Sex Fantasy, in the flesh. Dark Eyes himself.

Fuck me, he's so goddamn hot.

Without thinking, Stella opened her mouth and lifted a hand to her chest. She pulled at her shirt, hoping to get some air on her newly flushed chest. But it was no use. He had his shirt off and was laughing with one of his buddies. When he leaned to the side to grab a bottle of water, she had to keep from licking her lips.

Before she could blink, he was looking her way, that sexy smile on his face again. She blushed, mortified he'd caught her glaring at his chiseled abs.

She didn't even notice Todd stroll in.

"Looks great, Marco." He had his hands on his hips and was gawking at the stairs.

Stella jumped in before he could start asking questions.

"Um, so, you had some samples for me?" She cleared her throat and turned so Dark Eyes wouldn't see her red cheeks.

Marco reached out and patted Todd on the shoulder. "You're gonna love these."

Ever since she'd hired Marco and his crew, Stella noticed he had a nasty habit of looking to Todd for answers. Even though he saw who signed the checks and where all the money was coming from, the big man just couldn't seem to accept that this was Stella's house. It drove her nuts, but he was affordable, came well recommended, and his work was flawless.

Just nod and smile, Stella. Nod. And. Smile.

They took their time going over the samples, and Todd made a show of choosing some truly hideous yellow tiles for the bathroom. When Stella insisted on dark blue, Marco all but rolled his eyes while Todd shrugged and laughed it off.

Next came the kitchen, and Stella had her heart set on white.

"You don't want white." Marco chuckled, sliding the sample away. He then pulled out a grayish-brown tile that looked more dirty than anything else.

"That's nice," Todd chimed in, picking it up and pretending to drop it.

Marco laughed and nudged his arm.

Fucking boy's club.

"I'd like white," she repeated simply. "It'll play better against the dark blue cabinets. And did you ask about the counter? With the butcher-block breakfast bar?"

"Butcher block?" Todd spat, his face contorting into something between confused and disgusted. "We're not having butcher block on the counter."

"I tried to tell her, but…"

"Oh, man, you don't have to tell me."

Stella's blood was boiling, but just as she plucked up the courage to give the assholes a piece of her mind, Marco's phone rang. He held up a finger, and she nodded, letting him leave the room to answer the call.

Before Todd could say anything else to piss her off, she got up and walked away, going back out the front and to the side of the house to breathe.

How can they sit there and talk about me like I'm not even there? And even if I wasn't fucking there, they shouldn't be talking about me anyway. I'm paying for this house, dammit. I'm paying that asshole's fee, and I'm putting a roof over that moron's head. How fucking dare they—

"Hey, you okay?"

The voice came out of nowhere and made her jump. She stumbled, her foot finding a dip in the gravel where the workers' boots had stomped through the wet dirt. She was halfway to the ground when a hand grabbed her arm. Solid and steady, it lifted, and Stella held on tight until she was stable again.

"Oh my god, thank y—" She finally raised her head and was met with two smoldering eyes that left her speechless. He was standing just a foot away, with what looked like genuine worry on his face.

"S-sorry. Uh..."

Dark Eyes came closer and put a more gentle hand on her arm. "Are you okay? You seemed a little…upset." He lifted his other hand and offered her a Coke. "Thought you might like this."

"Thanks. I…thanks."

"I know it can be stressful. But we're on schedule."

"Oh, no. I mean, yes, it can be stressful. But I know you guys are doing amazing work. Really, I can't thank you enough."

"I'm sure you could," he said, his eyes on hers and a sly smile on his lips. "If you really tried."

Is he flirting with me right now? No. Don't be an idiot.

"Um...well, thanks again." Stella opened her can and took a sip.

"And about Marco..." he began quietly, leaning in close. "He can be a little old-fashioned. It sucks, but he pays the checks, ya know. And he's good at all this. You're in good hands with us."

He reached out again and touched her arm, his rough fingers lingering on her skin. Stella's mind flashed back to her dream, and she wondered how those calluses would feel against her clit.

Shit, Jenny was right.

His hands were big, and she couldn't help but picture them cupping her ass as his thick cock drove into her soaking wet pussy.

"Yeah," she coughed out, reddening at the thought of his naked body against hers. "It's just one of those annoying things, I guess. Some men don't like it when a woman tells them what to do. I think they find it emasculating. Like I'm holding their balls or something."

"Some men like that," he offered, lowering his voice. "Real men, that is. A real man would love it if you told him what to do. He'd probably get off on it. I know I would."

Stella almost choked on her soda.

What the fuck is happening?

He smiled and raised an eyebrow, his eyes wandering as she desperately tried to think of something sexy to say. But she was frozen in lustful shock.

"I mean, I would..." she tried, biting her lip.

"Babe?" Todd called from the front, oblivious as ever. "We good to go, or you wanna look at more tiles?"

Dark Eyes stepped back, his hand brushing dangerously close

to her right nipple, which was embarrassingly prominent through her light shirt. He winked and turned away, nodding to a clueless Todd as he passed by and went back to work.

Stella stood still, her panties wet and her pussy aching. Then she looked up at Todd and slumped.

"Tell Marco I want the white fucking tiles," she snapped before storming back to the car and cranking up the A/C.

five

. . .

STELLA WATCHED Todd wander back into the house. Her neck flushed as she thought about him and Marco, colluding to destroy her dream home. She gripped the wheel until her knuckles went white, then turned the key and pulled away from the curb.

As soon as she cleared the neighborhood, she dug her phone out of her bag and said, "Hey Siri, send a voice message to Jenny."

The phone obliged, and Stella took a deep breath before speaking.

"Jen, I'm gonna lose it. I swear to God, if one more man explains my own fucking house to me, I'm gonna throat punch someone."

She swerved around a slow-moving truck, muttering under her breath.

"I'm standing there—literally standing in *my* house, the one *I* paid for—and Todd starts making decisions like he's the one footing the bill. As if I'm just... I don't know, decorative. And Marco? He just laughs. Like we're all sharing a cute moment. Like I'm the nagging wife in a sitcom who wants something 'silly' like white tile, and the menfolk know better."

She braked harder than necessary at a red light, the car in front a little too close for comfort.

"Oh, and you're gonna love this. The second I stand up for myself? The second I say something they don't like? I get *the face.* You know the one. That smug little 'aww, she's emotional' look. I'm *this close* to setting the tile samples on fire and firing the whole damn crew. I'll finish the fucking thing myself if I have to."

The light turned green. She resisted the urge to honk at the slow-to-respond car ahead.

"And then—*then*, Jenny—the hot one shows up. Shirtless. Sweaty. Smiling like he knows exactly how hot he is. And I just… I malfunctioned. I stopped being a person and turned into one of those cartoons with the buggy eyes. I was two seconds away from fanning myself like a Victorian widow."

Stella pulled into the office lot and jammed the gear into park. She let out a breath, angry with herself for her lack of filter.

"I need professional help. Or a few margaritas. You decide."

She hit send and climbed out of the car, slamming the door with a satisfying *thunk.*

The office was cool and quiet, thank God. She hadn't been out long, so most of the staff were still at lunch.

"Hey, Stella," came a voice from the break room. Mia poked her head out, protein bar in hand. "You okay?"

"I'm great," Stella said, forcing a smile. "Why do you ask?"

Mia blinked. "Um… you're holding your keys like a weapon."

Stella looked down. Sure enough, her fingers were wrapped around them like claws, the longest key poking out between her knuckles.

She forced a laugh and dropped them into her purse. "Just one of those days."

Mia raised her brows but didn't push. "Well, if you want coffee, I just made a fresh pot."

"Thanks."

She walked back to her office, feeling the flush in her cheeks.

Once inside, she shut the door and dropped into her chair. Her purse landed with a thud, and her laptop screen sprang to life.

Work. She needed work. Data, schedules, clients, deliverables —give her something she could *control*.

Her phone buzzed. Of course it did.

Fucking Todd.

> Where did you go?
>
> You just left me here?
>
> You're acting crazy, Stell. I don't get it.
>
> Call me.

She turned it face down. It vibrated again.

> I just think it's rude to storm off like that when we're trying to make decisions together.

Stella let out a laugh.

"Together," she repeated aloud, the word acid on her tongue. As if Todd had done anything except show up and gawk.

She opened her email, scanned the inbox, and clicked into a spreadsheet. Rows of client names and payment schedules stared back at her. Usually soothing—right now, useless.

The phone vibrated again. And again.

She picked it up, stared at it for one long second, then powered it off and shoved it in the drawer.

Silence.

Peace.

Except… not really.

Because under the rage, under the frustration, was *him*. Shirtless, smirking, standing so close she could still feel the heat off his chest. He'd looked at her like he wanted to touch her—no, like he *planned* to. Like he was just waiting for the right moment to do it.

And that voice.

'A real man would love it if you told him what to do. He'd probably get off on it. I know I would.'

Her breath caught, and she clenched her thighs without meaning to.

"Nope," she whispered. "Not happening."

She stood up, walked to the window, and stared out at the trees, hoping the blue sky might clear her mind.

But she was pissed. She was turned on. And she was *very* much not over it.

Behind her, her laptop pinged—an email from a client needing advice on yet another large purchase.

That, she could do.

But the ache in her chest (and lower) wasn't going anywhere.

six

. . .

NO MATTER how hard she tried not to, Stella spent the rest of the day thinking about Dark Eyes.

She didn't even know his name, yet she couldn't help but feel drawn to him. And the way he came out after her to see if she was okay made her think he'd been watching her too.

He was definitely flirting back there. Right?

Meanwhile, she didn't speak to Todd for the rest of the day. When she turned her phone back on, she had a single text telling her he'd be at a friend's that night.

She didn't reply.

Jenny's right. This can't go on.

Knowing she'd have the house to herself helped calm her nerves some. Stella picked up supplies on the way home, including candles, wine, and ice cream. She ordered dinner, lined the shelves with tea lights, and poured herself a big glass of white zinfandel, drinking half before the fridge door had even closed.

Marco and Todd. That's what she was mad about. The tile, the butcher block, the way Marco always looked at Todd for approval —like she didn't even exist. That was what had her wound up. Not the dreamboat with the devastating smirk and porn star abs.

She refilled her glass, wandered into the bedroom, and turned toward the laundry pile, trying not to remember how it had felt when he touched her arm. It was just a gesture. Normal. Basic. Polite.

And yet she was still warm where his hand had been.

Ugh.

She dumped the laundry onto the bed, muttering to herself as she sorted. Work pants. Workout leggings. And way too many graphic T-shirts she refused to fold for Todd.

At the bottom, she found the blouse she'd been wearing the day she first saw Dark Eyes. She hadn't worn it to turn heads, but she'd noticed one or two of the guys watching her.

She stared at it. Then rolled her eyes and shoved it to the bottom of the pile.

You're obsessing. Get a grip.

Her phone buzzed on the nightstand. She grabbed it, expecting another passive-aggressive text from Todd. But it was from Jenny.

> Are we burning the tile samples or are you just
> going full cavewoman and living in the bathtub?

Stella smirked, plopped onto the bed, and tapped out a reply.

> Thinking about it. Either that or retiling the
> bathroom in Todd's bones.

The typing dots popped up immediately.

> Don't tempt me. Also, how hot is he in real life?

Stella stared at the screen, wine glass poised at her lips.

She could lie. Say he wasn't that cute. Say he was average. Say she wasn't even thinking about him.

But what was the use of that?

> It's bad.

Like "run into traffic" bad or "let him ruin your life" bad?

Stella dropped her head back and groaned.

> I think I need a priest. Or a cold shower. Or someone to tase me every time I look at him.

So... let him ruin your life. Got it.

Stella set the phone down, grinning despite herself. But the grin faded quickly. Because it *was* bad.

She didn't do this. She didn't get flustered. She didn't daydream about forearms and sweat and deep, raspy voices that said things like, '*A real man would love it if you told him what to do.*'

Stella stood up, took the rest of her wine with her, and headed to the bathroom.

Hot water ran into the tub, fogging up the room as she undressed. Stella wiped at the mirror and sighed. She looked like she'd run a marathon.

"This is fine," she told herself, pulling her hair into a bun. "This is fine. You're just... stressed."

But she wasn't just mad about the tiles. And she wasn't just annoyed with Todd.

She was turned on. Like there was a constant hum inside her unsatisfied core that, no matter what she tried, wasn't going away.

She pressed her hands to the tile wall and stepped into the water, letting the heat melt away everything else.

Everything except *him*.

seven

. . .

STELLA SANK DEEPER into the tub, steam curling around her face as she tilted her head back and exhaled. Maybe it was the wine. Maybe it was the way he looked at her like she was a challenge he *wanted* to lose. But as the heat wrapped around her body, her mind started to drift.

Just a little fantasy. A harmless one.

What if he were here?

The room softened around her as she closed her eyes, one hand grazing her thigh, the other swirling lazily in the water. Music played low in the background, the kind of sexy, slow rhythm that made her skin buzz.

She pictured him—Dark Eyes—standing across from her in the bathroom, casual and cocky and completely in control.

Him in jeans, barefoot. Her in nothing but a robe.

She felt a cool tingle when his hands found her neck, tracing his fingers along her collarbone. His lips were soft against her skin, and she let out a deep breath as he moved around her body, trailing kisses along her neck. He smelled like beer and lumber, and his hands were speckled with paint. For some reason, it drove her wild.

He licked along her jawline and found the corner of her

mouth, but before she could meet his lips, he stood to his full height, towering over her with lust in his eyes. His messy hair tumbled into his lashes as he gave her a look that made her clit pulse.

Stella tilted her head back and smiled when he took her face in his hands. The kiss was surprisingly soft, but she felt a smirk play on his lips when his hand reached her breast. He cupped and squeezed while his thumb ran over her nipple, bringing it to life with just a few strokes.

His other hand reached behind and pulled at the robe, revealing her naked and needy body. Then he was on her—his hands and his lips, kissing and squeezing like he just couldn't get enough.

Melting into his chest, Stella reached for him, quickly finding the button on his jeans. She unfastened the front, delighted to feel his cock straining to be freed. He stepped back, shuffling out of his jeans to reveal tight black briefs and a delicious bulge in the front. Smiling, he motioned for her to get in the tub.

She did as she was told, sucking in a sharp breath as her skin prickled from the heat. The room smelled of cinnamon and vanilla, and the candles flickered against the walls. Her body warmed, and her pussy ached, but she waited. Dark Eyes stood watching, shirtless and sexy and ready for her. His hands slipped under the briefs, pushing them to the floor, finally letting his cock pop free.

Stella clenched at the sight of it and ran her hands over her breasts, pinching her nipples as he stepped in behind her.

He slid into the water, his length dragging down her back until it rested between them. She felt his hands slip around her body, reaching for her breasts. He pinched at her nipples, tugging and twisting them between his fingertips, chuckling when she moaned.

"Oh!" she cried out. "Oh God."

Stella's head fell back onto his chest, giving him room to nibble her neck. Between his tongue on her earlobe and his hands on her tits, she was in heaven. And with the way her clit throbbed, she knew it wouldn't be long before she got her release.

Gently and slowly, his right hand dipped under the water and nestled between her legs. He danced around a little, tracing her thighs and the edges of her labia with each pass. The second he reached her opening, Stella sucked in a breath, wanting desperately to move his hand to her clit. But she let him play, sliding his fingers in and out while still working her nipple with his left hand.

"You want me to fuck you?" he whispered in her ear.

"God, yes. Fuck me," Stella breathed.

He immediately shifted his fingers from her opening and dragged them into place. They sat on either side of her clit in a V-shape, pressing and circling until her breath caught.

At the same time, he pinched and plucked at her nipples, sending shocks down to her groin. Finally, when she thought she couldn't take it anymore, his fingers came together, roughly rubbing her clit with hard and heavy strokes. And it didn't take long for Stella to feel her orgasm building. Not the short flutter from the night before. No. This felt big. This felt intense.

Dark Eyes worked her relentlessly—round and round, never missing a stroke. Then his other hand reached around, thrusting inside and pulling a groan from deep inside. Water splashed around them, and Stella's legs started to twitch. She gripped the edge of the tub and involuntarily shuffled back with every pulse inside.

Quickly, she reached for her nipple and tugged, knowing she was just a few strokes away from the release she so desperately needed.

"Cum for me," he growled.

And she did.

Stella roared out as the pleasure shot through her, her mind going fuzzy and her hips twitching. She rode the wave, panting and heaving in the water. After a minute or two, she was ready to fall, but something told her she could take more. As sensitive as she felt, she slipped the vibe back in place and kept going, pressing and grinding until she came again.

Exhausted, Stella sank back, her head hitting the edge of the tub and her shoulders plunging into the warmth. She caught her breath and turned off the vibes, pulling the second one free and tossing them both onto the towel on the floor.

She hadn't orgasmed like that in months. Even when she went solo, it was never this intense.

I gotta get that guy's name.

eight

. . .

one week later

WHEN SHE PULLED up to the house, Stella searched the front for any signs of her crush. He'd popped up in her dreams every night since they'd spoken, and she'd imagined him more than once as she got herself off.

He was like a magic trick: one smirk and she was throbbing.

In the car, she checked her hair and reapplied her lipstick before adjusting her tits to sit *just so* in the shirt.

A little cleavage never hurt, right?

Stella noticed more than a few pairs of eyes watching her as she strode up the path to the house. It made her feel confident. It made her think Dark Eyes might strike up another conversation.

But the moment she walked through the new front door, her good vibes vanished. Under the almost-finished stairs sat a mountain of boxes, and the pictures on the side were enough to make her want to scream.

"What the fuck?" she asked no one in particular, though one of the guys to her left looked up and shrugged. "What is all this?"

Ignoring the tarps and the paint, she marched over and grabbed the closest box.

Video games? Cables? Stupid comic book toys?

In a slight frenzy, Stella lifted and tossed aside a new silent-click mouse, an expensive-looking keyboard, and a memory foam footrest. From there, it only got worse. Monitors, desks, and a giant, ugly chair she could only assume was ergonomically designed for lazy assholes to lounge around in all day while their fucking girlfriends went to work and earned all the goddamn money.

Stella grabbed her phone and dialed Todd's number. He was supposed to meet her there, but was late, as usual.

"I'm like, five minutes away. Chill."

Chill?

She hung up and did her best to stay calm. But then Marco walked in with a massive smile on his face, which made her even more enraged.

"Stella, you made it. I assume you came to see the setup?" He slapped his hand on one of the boxes and rested his elbow on the corner. "I think Mr. Eddings will be *very* happy."

"Mr. Eddings? What are you talking about?" He'd never called her Miss-anything to her face, but fucking Todd got *Mr. Eddings*?

"Maybe we should wait? He's coming, no?"

"Marco." Stella sighed, a hand on her forehead. "Just show me what you're talking about. Please."

The big man shrugged and raised his hands as if to say, *Okay, okay. Whatever you say.* Then he turned on his heel and motioned for her to follow. They crossed under the stairs and into the hallway.

"When he called and said this room was a priority, I made sure the guys had it almost done for today. And I'm pretty happy with how it came out," Marco sang, stopping just short of brushing his shoulders with self-admiration.

He motioned to the right, where the guest room and ensuite bathroom were due to be. Across the hall, Stella had planned for a downstairs washroom and an office.

Or so she thought.

Marco pushed his hand through the plastic covering the door on the right and stepped through, holding it up so she could duck in herself. But she froze in the doorway.

"What do you think?" Marco smiled, raising his eyebrows and turning to face the windows.

Stella took a shaky step in, her head spinning. The walls were black, and they'd built a custom corner desk with shelves. Around the edges of the room were cheesy LED light strips, and the wall to her left was green. Gaudy, bright, obnoxious green.

"What the *fuck* is this?" Her voice was quiet and even, but her hands shook with rage. "Marco? This is supposed to be a guest bedroom. What is—"

"Mr. Eddings said you guys needed a room for his work. I think the green screen came out great, don't you?"

She wanted to scream. To claw the paint off the walls. More than that, she wanted to rip Marco's arms off and beat him to death with them.

"Todd asked you to do all this?" she managed to get out, her cheeks flushed and her voice weak.

"Of course." He smiled, glancing over his shoulder and out the front window. A car pulled up, hopping the curb like she hated. "Oh, there he is."

Marco hustled back into the living room to meet the man he obviously thought was in charge. Stella took one last look and followed. Her fingernails dug into her palms, and her knuckles went white.

I'm gonna fucking kill him.

The second she saw his face, Stella couldn't help but lunge. He was smiling and reaching for the boxes—boxes she *knew* she'd paid for. With her hands already in fists, she cocked her arm back and swung, taking the last couple of steps in a jog to add momentum. She connected with his jaw and felt hot pain in her hand. But she knew it was worth it when he cried out and fell back.

Not satisfied with a slightly red cheek, Stella grabbed one of the smaller boxes. She threw it at him, reaching for more and more until she couldn't physically lift anything else.

"You motherfucker! Who the *fuck* do you think you are? How fucking dare you change my house?! *My fucking house*, Todd!"

She charged then, grabbing his shirt and pushing him back until he tripped and fell. Stella went with him, her elbow crashing into the cement with a sickening thud. She cried out and rolled away—but not before reaching over and slamming her other fist into his groin.

At this point, they had a bit of an audience, and when she moved to grab him again, a hand held her back. He was gentle but firm enough to keep her still, whispering in her ear to try and calm her.

"He's not worth it."

Stella was too angry to let Dark Eyes get to her and pulled herself free. Todd stood too, and, this time, Marco got between them, his hands raised and a confused look on his face.

"Stella, you need to calm down. Don't be hysterical. I think there's just been a misunderstanding. When Mr. Eddings called me—"

"Todd *isn't* paying your fucking bills, Marco. I am! It's *my* fucking money and *I'm* the one in charge. No matter how much that pisses you off, you work for *me*—not him. You get that? You had no right to change my plans without consulting me. You had no right—"

Marco's smile turned sour, and his eyes narrowed as he pointed his finger in her face. "You should be careful there, Stella. I'm trying to be nice here, but if you don't watch what you say—"

All the months of frustration, exhaustion, and anger at the little comments caught up to her. Stella stepped forward and smacked the man across the cheek. He looked as shocked as she was, and then, to her surprise, he lunged at her.

She felt a hand on her arm, pushing her to the side, and Marco was on the floor in the blink of an eye. Dark Eyes stood over him, his fist still cocked and pure rage on his usually light and sexy face.

The room went quiet but for heavy breathing. Stella looked from man to man, wondering what the fuck to do now. She put her hand on her savior's arm and pulled him away, thanking him in a whisper. Finally, she stepped forward and raised her voice.

"You're fired, Marco. Get *the fuck* out of my house."

When he finally managed to get back on his feet, he laughed and snarled at her, "Good luck getting anyone to finish this shit-hole of a house. I'm gonna blackball you to every contact I've got. Vendors, contractors, even the fucking maids won't set foot on this property."

He spat at her feet and spun around, yelling at his guys to drop everything and leave. But before he left himself, he turned back and pointed his fat finger in Dark Eyes' face.

"You're fucking done."

For a minute, Stella thought he might reach out and snap the digit in half. But Dark Eyes stayed quiet, his face unreadable.

They watched Marco go, the men following with their heads low. No doubt they'd be back later to collect the equipment once Marco was through with his temper tantrum. She could only hope they wouldn't break anything out of spite.

With the adrenaline still running high, Stella turned her attention to Todd, who was standing dumbstruck in the same spot, a hand over his eye and blood on his cheek.

"We're through, Todd. You and me? It's over. I want you and your shit out of the apartment before I get home." She turned and walked away before he could respond, but stopped when she saw the gaming stuff.

"This stays. Since I'm pretty fucking sure you used *my* card to buy it all."

He didn't say anything, which was as good as an admission in her books. She left him bleeding and confused on the floor.

nine

. . .

SHE WAITED IN THE HALLWAY, listening as Todd got to his feet, called out for her, then huffed out the door, slamming it behind him.

For a few precious seconds, there was silence.

No yelling. No groaning. No boxes being hurled across the room.

Just silence.

Stella stood frozen, her chest still heaving. The adrenaline hadn't worn off yet, but the heat was already fading, leaving her cold. Her right hand ached from where it had collided with Todd's jaw. Her elbow throbbed, and her shoulder was stiff.

Slowly, she turned and looked at the mess in the ruined room.

The stupid chair. The LED lights. The goddamn green wall.

Her guest room.

She walked back in, crossing the floor with heavy feet. The room was supposed to be blue, with gorgeous hardwood and a lovely king-size bed for her folks to stay in when they visited. She'd even planted her mom's favorite flowers outside the window, so she'd see them every day.

It was supposed to smell like lavender and old paperback novels. She'd imagined her parents sitting in here — her dad reading the paper, her mom opening the curtains and smiling at the garden.

Now?

Now it looked like the inside of a sixteen-year-old's gaming dungeon.

She wanted to cry. It was all ruined. The room, the house. How could she get it finished now? Not with Marco planning to badmouth her all over town.

Stella pressed her hand to her mouth and collapsed onto the edge of the desk. Her knees bent, and she sank down until she was sitting on the floor, her back against the wall. The drywall was cool on her spine. She closed her eyes and let it hit.

The tears came slowly at first — one or two slipping down her cheek, warm and uninvited.

Then they multiplied.

She curled into herself, arms wrapped around her knees, and let the grief out in deep, broken sobs. It wasn't just the room. It wasn't even just today.

It was everything.

The months of second-guessing. The way Marco had too often called her "sweetheart." The way Todd laughed off her design choices, as if she were redecorating a dorm room. The passive-aggressive texts. The not-so-passive-aggressive credit card charges. The fucking projector.

She cried for all of it.

When the tears slowed, Stella wiped her face on the sleeve of her shirt and let out a shaky breath. Her head throbbed from the crying, and her throat felt raw. She was exhausted — emotionally and physically.

But under the wreckage of it all, there was still a flicker of fire.

She pushed herself up slowly, using the desk for support. Her legs were stiff, and her butt was probably covered in dust. She didn't care.

She walked out of the room, past the stupid stack of electronics, and into what should've been the kitchen — the shell of it, anyway. She grabbed a water bottle from the counter and chugged it, the plastic crinkling in her hand. Then she walked to the living room, looked at the front door, and locked it.

Just in case anyone else decided to barge in and destroy something.

Then she doubled back and marched toward the guest room again.

No hesitation this time.

She pulled down the plastic sheeting still covering the hallway, letting it fall in a heap. Her eyes fell on one of the boxes — a fancy-looking "ErgoPro" keyboard setup. She dragged it into the living room and tossed it against the wall.

Next was a monitor, followed by a goddamn helmet, which she punted across the room.

When she reached the green screen wall, she stood there for a minute, hands on her hips, breath short.

"I said blue," she muttered, eyes burning.

She looked around, found a screwdriver, and started yanking LED strips off the molding one by one. They tore like cheap ribbon. She bundled them in her arms and tossed them into the hallway.

The room didn't look much better afterward, but at least the glow was gone.

That helped.

A little.

Finally, she collapsed back into the desk chair and opened her phone to text Jenny.

> Todd and I are done.

Wait... what?

> He ruined the house, Jen. Had Marco change my guest room into a fucking gamer den

Did you kill him?

Is he dead? Do I need to bring a shovel?

Seriously, babe, I'm worried. Call me.

Stella smiled through the ache in her jaw. Her hand still shook a little, and she could feel the swell where her elbow had slammed into concrete, but her fingers were steady enough to reply.

He's not dead. But he won't be walking straight for a while.

Also, I fired Marco. Long story

Babe... shit

I'm ok. I'll call you later.

She set the phone down just as a door opened somewhere in the house. Not the loud click of the front. More like the temporary door they had in the back.

Shit. He came back.

Stella panicked. If Marco had come back, there was no telling what he might do. He'd already lunged at her, after all.

Desperately, she grabbed the screwdriver, her eyes scanning the room for another weapon.

She waited, the sound of heavy boots getting closer.

ten

. . .

"STELLA?" a voice said softly from the hallway.

She turned, wiping her cheek on her sleeve, breath catching when she saw him in the frame.

Dark Eyes.

He leaned against the wood, ankles crossed, arms folded. A small, sad smile tugged at his lips. She spotted the dried red on his knuckles and felt a sharp twist in her chest.

He lost his job because of me.

"Oh my god, I... I'm so sorry, uh..." she faltered, hoping he'd finish the sentence for her.

"Cal," he offered, his mouth curling just slightly. "And don't worry about it. Marco's a dick. Yeah, he's a decent contractor, but he's not exactly a team player. And you were right—he doesn't like taking orders from strong, independent, and incredibly sexy women."

Her heart was still hammering from the day's chaos. She blinked at him, not quite processing what he'd just said.

Sexy?

"I just..." Stella looked down at her hands. They were still trembling. Her knuckles throbbed, and a small, angry cut was starting to sting.

Cal stepped forward and gently took her hands in his. His grip was warm and grounding.

"Take a breath. It's okay."

She shook her head, trying not to cry again. "Is it? You don't have a job, and I don't have a finished house. So I don't really see how any of this is okay."

He tilted his head, that soft, unreadable look still on his face. Then he reached up and tucked a strand of hair behind her ear.

The second his fingers brushed her cheek, something cracked open inside her.

Not anger. Not grief. *Something else.*

Longing.

Stella felt her breath catch again—but for a very different reason.

"I don't know what I'm doing," she admitted, her voice barely a whisper. "I thought I had it under control, but everything just… collapsed."

"You didn't collapse," Cal said quietly. "You stood up for yourself. Loudly, and impressively, I might add."

He gave her a smile so full of warmth it made her want to crawl into his arms and never leave.

Then his gaze dropped to her hand.

"Shit," he murmured, stepping closer. "Let me see."

Stella looked down and winced. Her knuckles were red and slightly swollen, with a small split in the skin near the base of her index finger.

"You landed a solid hit, but you need ice. And probably something on that cut," he said, already turning toward the kitchen. "Sit."

She didn't argue.

A few minutes later, he came back with a small ziplock of ice and a dish towel. He crouched in front of her, wrapped the ice gently, and placed it in her hand.

"You've got a badass right hook," he said, adjusting the towel. "But let's not make a habit of punching people, yeah?"

Stella huffed out a laugh, her lips twitching. "I'll try to keep it classy from now on."

He smiled, but his eyes lingered on her elbow next. "Let me see that too."

She rolled up her sleeve, revealing an angry red scrape with the beginnings of a bruise.

"Damn," he muttered, softer now. His fingers brushed against her skin, and she felt the chill of the ice follow. "You went down hard."

"I didn't feel it at the time."

"That's adrenaline for you."

He stayed there a moment longer, holding the ice to her arm, his other hand resting gently on her thigh. The weight of it was comforting. Steady.

When he looked up at her, she lost all sense of self. All the hurt and anger just faded away.

She leaned forward and kissed him.

It was soft at first, but when he opened his mouth and let her in, she deepened it, her tongue sliding against his with slow, deliberate need.

His hand left her elbow, but the other didn't move, which made her pause.

"Shit," she whispered, pulling back suddenly. Her lips tingled, her heart racing. "Shit, I'm sorry. *Fuck*, I just... I—"

Cal chuckled and shook his head. That familiar smirk returned —devastating and crooked.

"Don't be sorry. I've wanted to do that since the day you showed up in that little blue dress." He paused, hand on his chin. "Actually, before that. But that dress really got my dick hard."

Fuck.

Stella bit her lip. She knew exactly the dress he meant. And yes, she'd worn it hoping he'd notice.

She swallowed hard, then surprised herself. "What else gets your dick hard?"

Cal raised a brow, delighted. "You're bold all of a sudden."

"I've had a day," she said simply, lifting her chin.

He stood, his right hand grazing her wrist and trailing up until it hovered at her chest. He curled his finger until she stood, then moved the chair away before slipping behind her, brushing his fingers across her spine.

"I like this. And I've been fantasizing about lifting that little black number over your hips so I can finally get my head between your legs."

The words shot straight to her core. She pressed her lips together to control her breathing.

"What else?" she asked, voice low.

"The way your fist connected with that shithead out there? That was pretty fucking hot." His voice grew darker, rougher. "The way you gave them a piece of your mind. Very demanding. I know it was a serious situation, but I couldn't help picturing you in heels and a tight, black lace number. Maybe some leather, too."

He circled back in front of her, eyes smoldering. He stared unabashedly at her cleavage, his tongue slipping out slightly as her chest rose and fell. Then he bit his lip and looked up to meet her gaze.

"When was the last time that moron made you moan?" he asked. "I mean, *really* moan. Head back, breath-catching kind of pleasure."

"Never," she said, barely audible.

"That's a damn shame. I might have to do something about that."

"You seem pretty sure of yourself," she said, trying to sound braver than she felt. Her palms were damp, her knees unstable.

"Tell me you haven't thought about it. About us." Cal leaned in slightly. "I've seen the way you look at me. You know, I don't usually go around shirtless on job sites."

He ran a hand through his hair, his bicep flexing under the sleeve of his T-shirt.

She hesitated, thinking back to every solo session he'd inspired.

Oh, what the hell.

"I've thought about it," she admitted with a shrug.

"Tell me," he said.

His hands lifted to the top button of her shirt. He waited.

Stella gave a small nod and drew a shaky breath.

"I've pictured us on the beach. I'm in a little bikini, and you're lying beside me."

Cal began undoing her buttons, one at a time, his brow raised in amused anticipation.

"You always start with my tits. Squeezing and cupping them a little before you…"

Her voice faded as he revealed her black lace bra.

Cal let out a low groan, his lashes dark as he looked down. "Keep going," he murmured, brushing his nose along her skin.

"Uh… you take my nipple in your mouth and suck. Your tongue is warm and soft, but… you're not always gentle."

He pulled the cup aside, exposing her hard nipple, and did exactly as she described.

"Fuck."

Her thoughts scattered. "You like to play. But you know I need more, and your fingers… they find their way… down."

He eased her toward the desk, pressing her gently until she sat back against it.

"You were saying something about my fingers?" he asked, already unbuttoning her tight jeans.

She nodded, breathless, and let him peel them down her legs. She stepped out of her shoes and socks, left in just her underwear and open shirt.

"Keep going," he said, his voice a command now. "What else do I do?"

"You… slip your fingers under my panties, and…"

Say it, bitch.

"I'm so fucking wet. You stroke from my pussy to my—oh!"

His fingers found her, warm and slick. He circled her clit, pressing just right, drawing a sharp gasp.

He kept at it, slow and deliberate, while she gripped the desk to stay upright.

"What else?" he whispered.

She couldn't speak. Instead, she tugged her bra down, baring both breasts. He took her in eagerly, mouth hot on her skin as his fingers picked up speed.

Inside her. Then outside. Over and over until she was panting, twitching, close.

His lips returned to hers, stealing a deep kiss, while his fingers drove her higher.

And then—

"Fuck—Cal—"

She cried out, her orgasm crashing over her in a tidal wave. He held her steady, never letting go, working her through it until her legs buckled and her gasps turned into soft moans.

"Oh my god," she breathed. "That was… incredible."

Cal smirked, reaching for his zipper.

"You're not done, are you?"

eleven

· · ·

STELLA COULDN'T THINK STRAIGHT. In the last hour, she'd fired the contractor on her dream house, broken up with her deadbeat boyfriend, and been finger-fucked by an impossibly sexy stranger.

At least now I know his name.

"Stella?" Cal hesitated, his zipper halfway down. "You're not done, are you?"

He repeated his question, sweetly giving her the chance to say *no*. But the smile on his face was too much to resist. And when she glanced down, she could see his cock begging to be set free. No way she was walking away from that.

"Wh-what about Marco?" she asked suddenly, throwing him off.

"I don't wanna fuck Marco."

"No, I mean—what if he comes back?"

Cal pushed the zipper all the way down and shifted his hips, letting his pants hit the floor around his boots. "Then he'll get one hell of a show."

At the sight of his tight black briefs, Stella's eyes bulged, and she couldn't help but lick her lips. She'd been dreaming of that cock for weeks, and it was finally within reach.

Without a word, Cal removed his pants and shoes, tossing his socks into the corner before pulling the T-shirt over his head. She could smell his spicy deodorant as he stepped in, a little sweat glistening on his shoulders.

"I gotta ask," he said quietly. "When you thought about this... how was it?"

Cal's hands lifted to her breasts and scratched around to the hook at her back. It came free in seconds but stayed in place. She was still wearing the shirt, which he slid his hands under, sending a shiver down her spine. The bra and shirt fell at their feet as he stroked over her shoulders.

Stella shivered and thought about the question. She wasn't sure how to answer, but something inside told her to be honest.

What's he gonna do? Say no?

"Sometimes you're gentle. You move inside slowly, letting me feel every inch as you fill me up."

The side of his mouth lifted as he trailed his fingers along her thigh, finding her damp panties and stroking lightly over the pink material. She used his eagerness to fuel her confidence and stood up straight, grazing her hand over the prominent mound in his briefs.

"And then sometimes you ram that thing into me so hard I think I'm gonna split in two."

She felt his dick twitch at her words and squeezed a little, looking into his eyes, waiting to see how he'd respond.

Half worried he'd be intimidated and leave—half worried he'd do exactly as she asked.

Did I really just say that?

In a rush, Cal grabbed her face and brought his mouth to hers. He kissed her like a long-lost lover, reuniting after years apart. Like he missed and craved and wanted nothing but her.

Then his hands were on her ass, lifting her legs until they were wrapped around his waist. She snaked her arms around his neck just before he dragged her away from the desk and pushed her flat against the wall. She felt his dick on her clit and moved her hips, hoping it felt as good to him as it did to her.

Stella felt him pull back, and she instinctively released her hold around his neck. Cal put his hands under her arms and lifted, bringing his lips to her nipple for a few quick strokes before dropping to his knees. She kept her legs tight around his waist, loving the strength in his hands as he lowered her to the ground.

Cal found her breasts again, his teeth nibbling as he thrust his fingers back into her panties. Stella called out the second he found her still-sensitive clit. He read her body and moved to her pussy, using his fingers to massage her opening.

She matched his enthusiasm by reaching between them and slipping her hand down his briefs.

"Oh fuck." She blew out an amazed breath when she finally got her hand on it. Wrapping her fingers around his long, thick, and throbbing dick, she felt a new ache, knowing that he would feel incredible inside.

She put her other hand on his chest and pushed him back, lifting herself until he looked up to see what was wrong.

"Fuck me. Now."

Cal grinned and stood, wrestling his briefs off while Stella removed her panties. She got on her knees, and her mouth fell open when she saw his length, standing to attention right in front of her eyes.

She couldn't help herself. Before he could get back on top, she grasped his dick and brought her mouth down, taking him almost all the way in on the first pass.

He tasted salty, and he twitched when her tongue flicked over the tip. Then she took him in again and had a hard time controlling her gag reflex. He hit the back of her throat, and she heard him groan her name. That was all the encouragement she needed. Stella sucked and licked and devoured him until she was out of breath.

His hand moved to the back of her head, moans and gasps rushing from his lips as she worked him. Cal gripped her hair when she picked up the pace, her right hand around his length and her left on his thigh for support.

To her surprise, Cal pulled back, his dick dropping from her lips, wet and hard and perfect. He lifted her chin and wiped her lip. His dark eyes were hard to read, the serious look on his face almost intimidating with her on her knees before him.

Cal read her mind and smiled, dropping to her level and dragging her onto his lap. Stella straddled his legs and rode his length with her pussy a few times before reaching between them and taking him in her hand once more. She nudged him into place and groaned. He was huge, and she'd never felt so good.

With her arms around his neck, she rode him until she felt the familiar pull of an orgasm rush to her stomach. Cal grasped her hips and caught her nipple in his mouth, tugging and licking as she lifted up and down.

Before she got too close, he moved his hands up, lifting her free. He gently nudged her to one side, and Stella found herself on all fours again. Only this time, she leaned down so her pussy was in the air—open, wet, and desperate for him to fill.

Cal's hand stroked over her skin, coming down on her right cheek in a loud smack.

"Oh!"

He spanked the other side, then she felt him at her opening. His pulsing dick slid in like it was made for her, but this time, he was in control. It started off slow, his hand spanking her ass every few strokes. Then he leaned in and put his hand in her hair, gripping tight as he drove into her, over and over, until she thought she'd lose her balance.

Stella could tell he was close as the pace picked up, and he grabbed her hips for support. But he didn't cum. Instead, he pulled himself free and lifted her leg, almost tossing her onto her back and pouncing on top.

She moaned when he found her nipple again. But she missed his cock and opened her legs wide, encouraging him to get in place.

Though he didn't need it, Cal took the hint. When he thrust in, his hand grazed her clit, making her back arch and her toes curl.

Cal took one final bite of her soft flesh before pushing himself up, coming to a stop on his knees. He lifted her leg with his free hand, hooking it over his hip. He used it for leverage as he fucked her hard and fast, his fingers dragging roughly over her aching, overworked clit.

But he didn't let up. He could tell she was close and pressed harder, pounding into her over and over until she screamed, her orgasm taking over completely.

Sensing she was too sensitive for more, he slowed his fingers, giving her a break. Still, he kept up his attack on her pussy until he, too, came in a rush of heavy breathing and grunting. He fell forward, catching himself on a powerful forearm as he twitched and shuddered before finally falling to her side in a heap.

The room went quiet, but for the sound of ragged and exhausted breathing. And for the first time since he'd told her his name, she thought about the fact that there was nothing but thin plastic in the window frames.

My new neighbors are gonna love me.

twelve

. . .

WHEN THEY FINALLY CAUGHT THEIR breath, Stella felt an odd wave of self-consciousness. She turned her back on him, sat up, and reached for her clothes, suddenly eager to hide her naked body—as though he hadn't just had his hands and mouth all over it.

After a couple of tries, she snapped her bra into place and tossed the shirt over her head.

Cal's hand found her thigh and squeezed.

"What's the rush?"

Stella glanced back and saw the look on his face. He was relaxed and totally at ease.

"I, uh... I..." she stammered.

He reached for her arm and gently tugged her back onto his chest.

"Not regretting it already, are you? At least let me buy you dinner before you decide I'm an asshole."

Stella laughed. "I guess I'm just a little embarrassed. I'm not usually so…"

"Helpful?" he teased, leaning up to kiss her. "Contrary to what you might think, most of us like being told what to do. It's *very* sexy being with a woman who knows what she wants."

"Yeah, well, not all guys are so... accommodating."

"Let me guess," Cal sighed. "*Mr. Eddings* didn't like it when you criticized?"

"That's kind of an understatement."

"Fuck him."

"I'd rather fuck you," Stella said without thinking, shocking herself.

What is this guy doing to me?

"Oh, you will," Cal said, running his hand over her ass. "And often. But I think maybe now we should get dressed. Like you said, Marco will be back at some point."

Just hearing his name brought back the pit in her stomach. The stress. The fear of the unfinished house. Of how to move forward alone.

What the fuck am I gonna do?

"Fuck," she whispered, rolling away, a hand to her temple. "I fired my contractor. How am I gonna find someone to finish this place?"

She hadn't really meant to say it out loud—not to him, not right now. But to her surprise, Cal cleared his throat and answered.

"Well, actually..." He dropped his eyes when she looked his way.

Is he nervous?

"That's kind of why I hung back. I mean, don't get me wrong. This was" —he motioned between them and grinned— "definitely what I wanted. But, uh..."

Stella waited, eyebrows raised.

"My brothers and I have been talking about starting our own company. Trav's an electrician and general handyman, and Jase is an all-rounder. He paints, builds, installs kitchens—the works. So, we've been toying with the idea of trying something together. Maybe now's the time."

His tone was casual, but she saw the flicker of vulnerability in his eyes. This wasn't just a pitch—it meant something to him.

They were still half-dressed and tangled in sex and sweat, and yet here he was, offering a solution to the chaos she didn't even know how to fix.

She glanced down—not at his face, but at his spent, still-thick cock, resting against his thigh—and her brain short-circuited for a second.

She thought about what they'd just done. About how badly she wanted to do it again. Would working together ruin that? Could she handle seeing him every day and not jumping him in every room of the house?

I guess, technically, he'd be working for me...

"Um," she began, still sorting out her thoughts. "I mean, I..."

"You know what? I'm sorry. I shouldn't have said anything. I totally ruined a nice moment and—"

"Wait, Cal. My only hesitation is... well, this. You just made me cum like I've never cum before. That was seriously the best sex of my life, and I... I want more. I want *you,* and I wanna see if you can top what you just did to me."

Stella blushed and shook her head. "Unless you don't—"

"Trust me," he interrupted. "I want that, too. I wanna wrap your body around mine and fuck you until you can't see straight."

She let out a shaky breath, equal parts relief and arousal.

"Okay. Good. But then... do you think you'll be able to, you know, work for me?"

Cal sat up and pinched her nipple playfully, the shock blasting straight to her core.

"Honestly? The only thing I'll have trouble with is not doing *this* every time you walk in the room."

His lips grazed hers, gentle at first. Then his hand trailed down her stomach, and his fingers found her—still soft, still wet, still wanting.

When they brushed her clit, she gasped.

"I think that's a yes," he murmured, sliding two fingers inside her.

Stella raised her leg, giving him better access, the anticipation crawling up her spine. She looked down and bit her lip at the sight of his cock growing hard again.

"For the last few weeks," he said, voice gravelly, "my cock's twitched whenever you walk by. I've thought about this" — he added a third finger and dragged them over her slick walls — "for fucking weeks. Wanting to bend you over and ram inside until you scream my name."

Cal pulled his fingers free and gently teased her clit, testing her sensitivity. When she moaned and dug her nails into his shoulder, he pressed harder, circling with just the right amount of pressure.

"So I guess..." he whispered, rising up so she had no choice but to fall back onto the floor. His fingers stayed in place, and she felt the tip of his cock at her entrance. "I guess you'll have to decide if this is something you can handle."

Stella's head tilted back, hips shifting to meet him.

His thrusts started slow—full and firm—and her whole body lit up.

"Tell me you want this, Stella."

She opened her eyes and locked onto his.

Dark Eyes. Fuck.

"I want this," she said. "*Fuck,* I want this."

Cal thrust harder, and Stella wrapped her legs around his waist, losing herself in him all over again—forgetting Todd, Marco, and everything else that didn't matter.

thirteen

. . .

STELLA LEFT the house a little unsure of what she'd agreed to. They started talking about Cal and his brothers possibly finishing the house. And then he was fucking her again, knocking any and all rational thoughts out of her mind.

Fuck me, that cock is a thing of beauty.

Just picturing it made her pussy ache. She was so enthralled that she had difficulty remembering anything they'd said. Well, other than the fact he thought she was sexy and wanted to... what was it?

'Bend you over and ram inside until you scream my name.'

She wanted that, too. More than she could believe.

When she arrived home, Todd was filling boxes. From the look on his face, she knew he figured they'd talk and she'd forgive him —like she always did. But Stella could still feel Cal's fingers in her hair, taste the saltiness of his cock, and feel the warm tingle on her ass where he'd spanked her.

Todd didn't stand a chance.

But, being a kind person, she let him stay the night—on the couch. The next morning, she waited patiently as he filled his friend's van and then handed her the keys. When she locked up and left for work, it was like a weight had been lifted off her shoulders.

The feeling didn't last. How could it? The house and Marco were still a huge worry, and no matter how well he fucked, she had no idea if Cal and his brothers could actually take over.

Stella tried to call Marco twice during the day. She didn't want him back on the job, but she needed to know where things stood. Were any deliveries due? Was there anything that needed doing right away? Hell, she needed to know if she owed him money.

He'll call back for that if nothing else.

Her day came and went without hearing from Marco or Cal— and that made her stomach twist into knots.

Shit. Shit, shit, shit.

She walked into her now-empty apartment and paused, listening. No TV murmuring from the other room, no random video game noises, no passive-aggressive comments about how she'd arranged the kitchen.

For the first time in months, the space felt like hers again.

And it felt weird.

She kicked off her shoes and padded to the kitchen. Her fingers curled around the edge of the counter, and she stared at the spot where Todd's energy drinks used to sit in a crooked little pyramid, as if that counted as cleaning up after himself.

He's really gone.

The thought brought a flutter of relief, followed by a wave of exhaustion. She grabbed a glass, filled it with water, and took it to the couch. Sinking into the cushions, she pulled a blanket over her legs and leaned her head back.

In less than forty-eight hours, she'd fired her contractor, kicked out her boyfriend, and finally stopped pretending that everything was fine when it wasn't.

Part of her felt proud. But a bigger part was pure panic.

She chewed her cheek, thinking about Cal.

Three random men can't finish that house.

She hated herself for it, but Stella picked up her phone and opened a browser tab.

Local contractors near me.

There were plenty of listings. She scrolled past the ads, squinting at websites that hadn't been updated in years. Most were booked solid. A few offered *"free quotes"* but warned of 4–6 week wait times. She clicked into one that looked halfway decent and hit the contact button.

It rang twice before a woman picked up.

"Hi, um—hi," Stella stumbled. "I'm looking for someone to take over a residential project. My previous contractor walked off the job, and it's kind of time-sensitive."

"Sorry to hear that," the woman said, uninterested. "We're booked until mid-August. You can fill out a form on our website, and someone should get back to you."

Click.

Stella sighed and called another. And another. They were either booked up or didn't answer.

She tossed the phone aside and stared at the ceiling.

Cal.

Just thinking his name made her tense in all the right places. And he hadn't pressured her. He hadn't even offered himself outright—just mentioned he and his brothers were thinking about starting their own thing. That was all.

But she knew what he'd meant. The offer was there. And based on the way he touched her, kissed her, and wrecked her on the floor of her guest room, there was no way he wouldn't say yes if she asked.

And that was the problem.

What if she said yes, and they weren't up to the task? What if she ended up hating their work—or worse, feeling like she couldn't speak up because things between her and Cal were already so… intimate?

She couldn't afford to let sex cloud her judgment, not with her house. Not after everything she'd put into it. She also couldn't afford to waste another three months waiting on someone else.

But a little voice in the back of her head wouldn't let up.

You don't even know if they can pull this off. And you've only known him for five minutes.

And yet… something about Cal made her want to trust him. Not just with her body. With the work. With the vision. Maybe it was how he'd jumped in to defend her without hesitation. That he'd lost his job because of her. Or maybe it was how seriously he'd looked at the unfinished walls, like he was already planning their next steps.

Maybe it was just the way he said her name.

The apartment was quiet again, her phone screen dark on the table.

She didn't know what to do.

fourteen

. . .

THE NEXT MORNING, Stella stood at the bathroom mirror, dabbing concealer under her eyes and wondering if it was possible to be both exhausted and high on hormones at the same time.

Because *damn*—her body felt like it had been rewired. Her brain? Completely fried.

She swept on some blush, tossed her hair into a messy bun, and grabbed her phone just as it started ringing.

"Marco?"

"You say his name a lot," Cal joked. "Should I be worried?"

Stella laughed. "Shit, sorry. No. I've just tried to reach him and he isn't answering."

Cal stayed quiet for a beat.

"Um… what's up?" she asked.

He cleared his throat. "Well, I'm at your house. Looks like Marco and the team have been and gone. They took their shit and left you a bill on the counter."

"Right. Great."

They were quiet for a second. Then Cal asked, "I thought maybe you could meet me here? After work?"

Stella held in a breath. His voice was calming, but she could

61

hear the tiniest thread of hesitation beneath it. Nerves. He was trying not to overstep.

For some reason, that made her like him even more.

"Yeah," she said eventually. "I can be there around six, if that works for you?"

"Six is perfect. See you then."

———

Work dragged.

Her inbox was overflowing, her boss was extra chatty, and every time Stella managed to focus, her brain offered up a mental image of Cal shirtless. Or naked. Or pinning her to a wall with those arms...

By the time five-thirty hit, she was practically vibrating. She left the office, stopped for a couple of decaf coffees and pastries, and pulled up to the house at 5:59 on the dot.

There were no cars in the driveway, but a lone truck was parked to the side. She hesitated before getting out. Her palms were suddenly sweaty, and her chest felt tight.

What if last night was a one-time thing, and he regrets it?

Too late now.

She walked up the path, stepped through the front door, and spotted him near the kitchen.

He looked up and smiled. "Hey."

"Hey," she echoed.

Stella walked over, holding up the coffees and food. She placed them on the table and took a step forward, about to go in for a hug. But Cal raised his hand like he was offering a handshake.

They both froze, then laughed at the same time.

"Oh my God," Stella said, grinning. "Are we—what are we doing?"

"I have no idea," Cal admitted, scratching the back of his neck. "I figured it was safer to go professional?"

"You literally had your dick in my mouth yesterday." She smirked. "I think we're past professional, don't you?"

He choked out a laugh. "Fair point."

"Okay, let's start over," she said, stepping closer. "Hi."

"Hi." He wrapped his arms around her like he meant it—firm, warm, steady. Just enough to make her chest ache in a way that had nothing to do with sex.

"Thanks for coming," he said, pulling back.

She shrugged and looked around. "You said it all looked okay?"

Cal nodded. "Yeah. Sorry I just let myself in, but I was curious. Wanted to make sure nothing was broken or sabotaged. You know. In case Marco decided to be a final-grade asshole on his way out."

"And?"

He nodded toward the hallway. "Come on, I'll show you."

He led her through the house, pointing out that all the tools were gone, the floors were clean—well, *contractor* clean—and no wires had been yanked or drywall smashed.

"Guest room's untouched," he added, pausing near the stairs. "They left the mess. And the green."

Stella snorted. "I'm repainting that wall myself if it kills me."

Back in the kitchen, Cal picked up the envelope on the makeshift counter.

"This was left on top. Hope it's okay—I took a look. Doesn't look like he stiffed you, which is a shock."

Stella took the envelope, flipping it open to check. The total wasn't pretty, but it wasn't unexpected either.

"Yeah," she said. "That's about what I figured."

Cal leaned against the wall, arms crossed, watching her. "You okay?"

Stella mirrored his posture, leaning back on the counter. All at once, it was more real than ever.

"I don't even know. Did I really do the right thing here? Maybe I overreacted."

Cal came closer. "You fired a guy who disrespected you and kicked out a freeloader. Sounds like the right direction to me."

She looked up at him. "It's all happening so fast."

He smiled, warm and calm. "Then we'll take it one thing at a time."

"That's... weirdly comforting."

"I'm good at that." He tilted his head. "And also other things."

She smirked. "Yeah, I've noticed."

He closed the gap between them, wrapped his arms around her waist, and pulled her close so he could whisper in her ear.

"Don't worry. I got you."

She let her head fall back onto his shoulder. "If you say so."

They stood like that for a moment—her wrapped in his arms, him breathing slowly against her neck—before he pulled back slightly, resting his hands on her hips.

"I should probably tell you," he said, brushing a lock of hair from her cheek, "I, uh... invited my brothers over."

Stella blinked. "Here? Now?"

He nodded. "Yeah. I thought maybe they could give you the pitch. Let you see what we're about. If that's okay?"

She stepped back a little, eyeing him. "Wait. Really?"

Cal shrugged, almost sheepishly. "You thought I was lying about them?"

"Wha—no. I just kind of assumed there'd be a bunch of back and forth and a timeline and... I don't know. Meetings."

He grinned. "Look, we're obviously not a giant crew with branded vans and a warehouse full of fancy equipment. But we're not amateurs either. Trav and Jase are just finishing up a place across town. It's basically done. Another couple of days and they're out." He paused, his smile softening. "We're all yours."

Stella couldn't stop the smile that spread across her face. "You're really serious about this."

"I am," Cal said. The teasing edge was gone from his voice. "This isn't just some rebound project for us. We've been talking about going out on our own for a while. I just didn't expect it to happen right now."

She laughed, a blush creeping up her neck. "So… you're saying me losing my shit in the guest room was fate?"

He shrugged again, but this time his expression was more serious. "I'm saying I was in the right place at the right time. And maybe that wasn't an accident."

Stella looked up at him, her heart doing something funny and unfamiliar. It felt dangerously close to hope.

"How long before they get here?" she asked.

Cal looked at his watch. "Well, I wanted to talk to you first. So I told them seven."

Stella lifted his wrist to check the time. It wasn't quite six-thirty.

"So we've got time…" she whispered.

fifteen

. . .

CAL FURROWED his brow for a split second, then grinned.

He'd been on her mind all day—images and memories of his hands and dick taking over her every thought. She was more than ready for him.

Dropping to her knees, Stella fumbled with his jeans, tugging and pulling until they fell. The briefs followed soon after. His dick was already hard, springing up to greet her. She caught it in her mouth within seconds.

"Fuuuuuck," Cal groaned as she swirled her tongue over the tip.

Stella placed one hand on his ass and used the other to hold his length steady. She licked from base to tip, then took her time with his balls, drawing a gasp when she sucked one into her mouth.

Eventually, she focused back on his cock, bobbing her head until he was as deep as she could manage. She noticed his hands gripping the table and smiled, working him faster, harder, until she heard his breath catch.

Seconds before she thought he'd cum, he cupped her chin and guided her to her feet. His lips crashed into hers as he pulled down her pants and grabbed her ass. Then he spun her around until she was bent over the counter.

His hand came down hard on her ass, and she let out a cry of pleasure. She tensed when his fingers slid over her panties, which were already soaked. He touched her carefully, mumbling to himself as he stroked her slickness, then spanked her again.

Stella felt him grip the thin material and tug it to one side. His cock came fast and deep, slamming into her and pulling a moan from both of them.

Cal thrust with quick, punishing rhythm. She clung to the counter for balance, moaning louder when he slipped his hand beneath her shirt. She arched into him, offering up her breast. He pinched and tugged her nipple without mercy.

It wasn't long before she heard him panting, the sound getting sharper as he reached his peak. Cal came hard, grunting against her back, his body twitching from the release.

For a second, Stella felt a flicker of disappointment—but Cal wasn't done.

He spun her around, grabbed her clit, and went straight to work. His mouth latched onto her nipple again while his fingers thrust roughly inside her.

Her breasts heaved as her orgasm started to build.

"Oh, fuck. Fuck, Cal," she gasped as his thumb pressed firmly over her mound.

Between his fingers inside her, his thumb on her clit, and his teeth teasing her nipple, Stella came hard. Even through the release, he kept going—pushing her into another wave, then another, until she cried out again, completely undone.

Cal expertly stroked her G-spot, drawing the orgasm out until her whole body twitched. When he finally pulled free, Stella was limp, her hands still braced on the island, her mind an absolute blur.

He put a hand on her face and kissed her, trailing his fingers over her clit one last time, making her stomach spasm again.

She let out a breathless laugh. "You know," she managed. "I almost thought yesterday was a fluke."

Cal chuckled and reached for some paper towels. He handed a few to her and wiped himself clean before zipping back up.

And a gentleman, no less.

"I'd love to take the credit, babe," he said, finding her nipple through her shirt. "But I think this is all you."

"Oh, come on. I'm pretty sure you've got a trail of women with swollen, dripping pussies behind you."

Cal lifted her chin until their eyes met. "I'm serious, Stella. You just... you do something to me."

A flutter hit her stomach, sharp and deep, followed by a warm throb where she still tingled from his touch.

"Well, I'm glad. And I think you already know you drive me crazy."

Once she was cleaned up and redressed, Stella washed her hands and ran them through her hair.

"So, what now?" she asked, more to herself than him.

Cal glanced at his watch, then out the front window. "Well, assuming we don't traumatize my brothers by accident... we're gonna talk shop."

She gave him a look. "Right. The pitch."

"No pressure," he added quickly. "You're allowed to say no."

"That's not what I'm worried about," she said, adjusting her shirt. "I'm just thinking about what would've happened if they'd shown up five minutes ago."

Cal grinned and slid his hands around her waist. "Yeah. Probably should've put a sock on the door."

sixteen

. . .

IN THE END, they had to wait another twenty minutes before Cal's brothers arrived. The awkwardness from earlier quickly returned, and Stella suddenly realized they hadn't really had a normal, fully clothed conversation before. Making small talk felt too forced after having his dick in her mouth, so she made herself busy wandering the house and checking on the yard.

Cal spent the time awkwardly staring at his watch and glancing out the window, clearly embarrassed that they were late. He called one of them ten minutes in, his voice hushed and frustrated.

He hung up a minute later. "They're almost here. Some accident held them up. Sorry."

"It's fine." Stella smiled and took a step closer, then thought better of it. There was no way she could casually kiss him without wanting to slip her hand into his jeans.

Mercifully, a truck pulled up out front before she had to ask him his favorite color.

Cal hustled outside, but Stella held back, watching through the plastic window as he greeted the two men on her unfinished driveway. They clasped hands and bro-hugged before he turned and pointed at the house. The pair smiled and nodded, looking impressed. Then they came inside.

Fuck. Me.

They were about level in height, with the blond standing maybe an inch or two taller. All three were buff and solid, their arms tanned and toned from manual labor. Each wore jeans, though the darker-haired one had on a buttoned shirt, while Cal and the blond wore simple T-shirts. They had more or less matching work boots, which made her smile, like their mom had dressed them to match.

When they stood in a row, she was taken aback by how goddamn sexy they all were. Nothing boyish about this trio. They looked similar, yet each had his own distinct features. She assumed the blond was the youngest, since the darker one had flecks of gray in his hair. Cal had a couple near his sideburns, but not as many. All three had brown eyes that smoldered down at her.

Stella felt her neck flush. It wasn't every day she was faced with three big, beautiful men waiting for her approval.

Dear Penthouse…

"Hi." She waved awkwardly and glanced at Cal for a cue.

"Travis," he started, motioning to the blond. "Jason. This is Stella."

She smiled, unsure if she should shake their hands or curtsey. Travis took the lead, stepping forward with his hand outstretched.

"Nice to meet you, Stella. This place is amazing."

"Thank you." She blushed when his eyes locked on hers. He ran his free hand through his blond hair, and she quivered. "I had some help."

Jason came next and took her hand, too. It was warm and rough, just like Cal's.

"Jase. Nice to meet you."

He smiled. Or was it a smirk? Either way, it was hot as hell.

"Jase, hi." Stella grinned at them, then turned her eyes to Cal. He looked nervous.

"So," Travis said, clapping his hands together, "Cal filled us in on everything. Really shitty about your ex."

Nodding, Stella could only hope Cal hadn't filled them in on *everything*.

"And I'm guessing you're a little worried about us," he went on, ducking his head and rubbing the back of his neck. Like Cal, his bicep bulged as he spoke. "I mean, you don't know us. We get that. But we've been doing this a while, and we know we can finish this house for you. We actually have…"

Travis trailed off and nodded to Jase, who reached for his phone. Cal stepped forward, his hands in his pockets, shoulders raised slightly.

"Ah, here," Jase said eventually.

He turned his phone and handed it over. At his side, Travis was already scrolling on his.

Stella took the phone and looked at the picture. It was a kitchen. Big and expensive. It looked gorgeous, and when Jase leaned over and swiped to the left, the angle changed, giving her a close-up of the sink and countertops.

"This was my last job. You can keep scrolling to see more."

She did, looking at the pictures with wide eyes and a growing smile. It was good work. Better than Marco's, even.

"Here," Travis said, handing her his phone. "Some of my handiwork."

This is too cute.

Stella couldn't help but smile. These big, tough guys were showing her their work like they were back in school. She'd been nervous, but it was clear this meant a lot to them. And luckily, their work spoke for them.

Cal stayed quiet, letting his brothers take the lead. She could see he didn't want her to feel pressured to say yes just because they'd had sex. And the truth was, she had been worried about that. But if the pictures were anything to go by, she was in six very good hands.

Very large, very sexy hands.

"I think I've got some great ideas about the patio," Travis added. He chewed his lip and waited for her to speak, peeking at his brother as she mulled it over.

"Your work looks amazing, and I would love it if you guys could finish my house. But—" Stella held up her hand to temper their excitement. "What about what Marco said?" She looked at Cal, fingers twisting together. "He said he'd blackball me to his vendors."

Travis laughed and shook his head. "He's all talk. Besides, we know all the vendors. I've worked with pretty much everyone in this town. I guarantee they'd rather help us out."

"Okay then." Stella grinned and held out her hand so Travis could shake it. He looked surprised that it could be so easy, but grabbed her hand before she could change her mind.

Jase clapped his hands and high-fived Cal before asking if they could take a look around. They asked her for her plans and about the boxes Todd had ordered. They wandered, excitedly pointing things out to each other and occasionally asking her about unfinished areas.

Stella tugged on Cal's shirt when they went upstairs, holding him back.

She lowered her voice. "We need a contract. *Before* work starts. I don't want… this"—she gestured between them—"to complicate things. I need to know you're not gonna walk off the job if I don't call you back."

He looked surprised—and maybe a little hurt—but then he grinned. "Why wouldn't you call me back?"

Stella rolled her eyes. "I'm serious, Cal. I can't afford to keep—"

"I'll have something drawn up tomorrow," he said. "You can look it over, and we'll get started whenever you're ready. We've already got a crew in mind, and I'll spend the next couple of days getting the boys caught up. If that's all okay?"

Shit. Is it okay?

Now it was Stella chewing the inside of her cheek. Was this really a good idea?

"Do they know? About us?"

Cal shook his head and glanced up—his brothers' voices were getting louder. "Not a thing. And I won't say anything if you don't want me to."

"I just don't want them thinking I'm some kind of whor—"

"This master is awesome," Jase's voice boomed in the empty space.

Stella stepped back, putting some healthy distance between her and Cal.

Jase went on, oblivious. "Seriously, I wanna move in. Can I move in?"

"Sure. You just need to fix that fucking guest room first."

Cal's brothers took the stairs quickly, smiles all around.

"They got a decent amount done, but obviously, they're barely halfway there," Travis noted, running his hand over the unfinished drywall.

Cal cleared his throat. "I was just saying that we'll go over the plans tomorrow, and we can probably get papers signed and the guys here on Monday." He looked at Jase and Travis, who nodded enthusiastically.

"You mind if we look around some more? Maybe take a couple pictures?"

"Sure," Stella said, waving a hand to the side. "Mi casa es su casa, right?"

The second the boys turned toward the office, Cal wrapped his arms around her, pulling her out of the hall. One hand lifted to her chest, the other slid down her pants.

His lips brushed the skin behind her ear as he whispered, "I won't say anything. But I can't promise I'll be able to keep my hands off you."

He was on her clit again—gentle, slow. Even as his brothers' voices faded in and out, Cal pinched her nipple through her shirt and moved his other hand further, reaching for her opening.

But Stella grabbed his wrist. If he got too far, she didn't think she'd be able to stop herself.

"I want your hands on me as often as humanly possible," she whispered. "But maybe we should save it for when we have doors?"

seventeen

. . .

"I'M SORRY. But you can't just text me all that shit then sit here casually sipping coffee like that's normal," Jenny huffed, gripping her latte like a weapon. "Girl, what the *actual* fuck."

Stella winced. "Okay, to be fair, I *did* say it was a long story."

Jenny leaned in like she was about to hear a war story. "And now I'm here. So *tell it.* You fired Marco *and* broke up with Todd in the same twenty-four-hour window? Are you trying to make me orgasm from sheer joy?"

"I guess I just snapped," Stella muttered. "You've been telling me to cut the cord for months, and I knew you were right. I just... I don't know. I felt like I owed him or something. He was there when I first got the loan, you know? He cheered me on."

Jenny snorted. "Cheered you on? He was rooting from the couch while you did everything. He contributed nothing but crumbs in your bed and a trail of empty Red Bulls."

Stella laughed, despite herself. "Okay, *harsh*, but not wrong."

Jenny leaned forward, eyes wide. "Please tell me you got in his face. Tell me you gave him a piece of your mind."

"I hit him, Jen," Stella whispered, ducking her head. "Like... I actually punched him. And threw stuff."

Jenny gasped, clutched her chest, then slammed her hand on the table. "I've never been prouder. And Marco?"

"I slapped him."

Jenny's eyes widened. "Girl. *Girl*. I'm so fucking proud of you."

Stella grinned, then looked down at her coffee, stirring it slowly. "It felt good. And also totally insane."

"You've been *too nice* for too long. You let both those losers camp out in your life rent-free. You snapped, and good for you."

"I don't know. I mean, Todd had to go, and Marco *was* kind of an asshole…"

She looked up at Jenny, who was still beaming with pride. But Stella wasn't sure how much to tell her. Jenny already knew about *Dark Eyes* and Stella's little crush. But the rest?

Did it even really happen?

Her body still buzzed from his touch, but the longer she spent away from him, the less real it felt. He'd wanted her then and there—no doubt about that. The way he touched her had been strong and needy, and she'd believed him when he said he'd fantasized about her.

But that didn't make him a good guy. He made her cum, but could he make her happy? Did he even want to?

The truth was, even Stella didn't know what *she* wanted. Because as delicious as his dick was, a bigger part of her was too worried about her house. And if Cal couldn't pick up where Marco left off, she was totally fucked—in the worst way.

Jenny clocked the look. "But? There's a *but*. What's the but?"

Choosing to keep the *Cal* part of the story to herself—for now—Stella smiled.

"Well, Dark Eyes kind of got between me and Marco. And after everyone left, he said he and his brothers could finish the job. They're all in construction, and he seemed pretty confident. So…"

She took a breath and smirked. "I met them yesterday. They're dialing in an estimate this weekend. I'll see them again on

Monday, and if it looks good, they'll hopefully be able to get the place finished."

Jenny blinked, processing. "So let me get this straight. Your hot mystery man turns out to be a contractor *and* a knight in toolbelt armor?"

Before Stella could answer, Jenny reached across the table and squeezed her wrist.

"Are his brothers as sexy as he is? Please tell me they're as sexy as he is."

With a chuckle, Stella threw her friend a bone. "Jen, you don't even know. They're all gorgeous. Like GQ cover model, Insta-influencer, *romance novel cover* gorgeous. Tall, tanned, and toned."

Jenny's eyes nearly rolled back in her head. "I think I need to meet these boys."

"Aren't you dating that guy from work?" Stella raised a faux-disapproving eyebrow.

"First of all, he's not from work. He just happens to work in the same building. And second, we're not married. He's nothing more than a one-date dude right now. He definitely doesn't have dibs on me. So you need to ask if the brothers are single. Because if they look anything like Dark Eyes, I'm in. I'm so fucking in."

Stella laughed again, but her cheeks flushed. She'd forgotten she'd sent Jenny that sneaky picture of Cal—the one in the yard, backlit by the afternoon sun, water bottle in hand, shirt clinging to his chest. She'd snapped it quickly after Jenny text-yelled *SEND ME A PHOTO OR I'M COMING OVER.*

"Maybe let me see about my house first? Then I'll ask if either of them is DTF. Okay?"

"Ugh." Jenny groaned, but she was smiling. "I guess me and my pussy can wait."

eighteen

· · ·

STELLA SPENT most of Saturday cleaning.

The house wasn't finished—far from it. The frame was up, and most of the drywall had been hung, but there were still entire sections left exposed. The roof was just a tarp stretched tight, flapping faintly with every gust of wind, and there was a constant smell of sawdust in the air. Wiring had begun but wasn't complete. No floors yet, either—just plywood and chalk markings for future walls and furniture.

Still, it was hers. Her mess. Her dream.

She started in the front room and worked her way back with a broom, clearing piles of dirt, wood shavings, and tiny nails into a dustpan. At some point, she paused in what would be her office and let herself picture it finished: wide desk, bay windows, a little reading nook built into the corner, and a wall of bookshelves that reached all the way up.

It had taken years to get here.

She hadn't needed to borrow much. Her job paid well—better than she ever expected when she started—and she'd saved for a long time. The lot had been a good deal, too, and once she'd committed, she'd gone all in. No turning back.

This wasn't just a house anymore. It was a line in the sand.

Her own space, built exactly how she wanted it. No roommates. No boyfriends. No compromises.

When her phone buzzed on the makeshift counter in the kitchen-to-be, she wiped her hands on her jeans and checked the screen.

Cal.

Hey. Just checking in. You okay?

> I'm good. Just at the house. Cleaning up a little.

You don't have to do that. Wait for us.

> I want to. Helps clear my head.

She tossed the phone aside and got back to it, lugging out another trash bag of scraps and breaking down empty boxes. She didn't expect another text, but half an hour later, she heard the crunch of tires outside. A minute after that, Cal's truck door slammed.

He appeared in the doorway with a pizza box in one hand and a six-pack dangling from the other.

"I come bearing gifts," he said, stepping inside. "Figured you wouldn't take a break otherwise."

Stella smiled and gestured at the clean-ish work site. "You figured right."

They sat cross-legged on the floor, using an overturned crate as a table. Cal cracked open two beers and passed one her way.

"Non-alcoholic," he promised. "The place looks different without all the tools and garbage."

"Still a long way to go."

"Yeah, but you've done a lot. You should be proud."

"I am." Stella nodded. "I've worked hard for it. I've got plans for everything. A garden out back, a full outdoor kitchen, even one of those pergola things. And the office?"

She turned and waved her hand in the general direction. "I

want a window seat and books on either side. And a cozy little lamp overhead. Maybe a tiny coffee bar in the corner."

Cal looked around the unfinished room and smiled. "Sounds amazing."

"I've seen so many places that just didn't feel like me," she said. "Apartments, rentals, houses Todd thought were 'fine.' But this? This is me. All of it."

Cal took a sip of his beer, then smiled. "Then don't compromise."

"I won't."

"You don't have to," he said. "Not with us. We'll build it exactly the way you want it. No shortcuts. No bullshit."

She looked up at him, trying not to get emotional.

"I mean it," he said.

Stella reached for her beer and clinked the neck of her bottle gently against his. "To no compromises."

"To exactly what you want."

As the last bits of light faded outside, the house grew quiet. They'd eaten, talked, and laughed until the pizza box was empty and the beer was down to the final bottle. Cal leaned back against one of the half-finished walls, legs stretched, arms folded. Stella sat on the floor nearby, her eyes on the tarp ceiling that fluttered every time the wind picked up.

"This is gonna be beautiful," he said, voice low.

She looked at him and smiled. "It already is."

He glanced over. "Not exactly how most people would describe exposed beams and a ceiling made of plastic sheeting."

"Yeah, but most people didn't design it." She hugged her knees. "Every inch of this place is mine. Not just the layout or the finishes. I picked this lot. I chose the floor plan. Every choice, every nail, it's part of something I built for myself."

He smiled softly and stood, brushing crumbs off his jeans. Then he offered her a hand. She took it, and he pulled her to her feet with ease, steadying her with his hands on her waist.

"We'll build it right. I promise. No cutting corners. No compromises."

He leaned in and kissed her—just a brush of lips.

"I'll see you Monday?" he said, grabbing the empty box and bottles.

She nodded. "Yeah. Monday."

He opened the door but paused, glancing back. "Try not to clean the whole place before then, okay?"

She grinned. "No promises."

And then he was gone, the door swinging gently shut behind him, leaving her in her half-finished dream house, her heart a little full and her cheeks a little sore from smiling.

nineteen

· · ·

MONDAY CAME QUICKLY, and Stella felt a buzz of nerves as she drove to the house. She knew Cal and his brothers had been there Sunday, going over plans and talking through the job, but the idea of sitting down with all three of them still made her stomach flutter.

Given how drawn she was to Cal, would it be weird to act like his boss?

Or maybe he'd get off on it?

The last time she'd seen him, they hadn't done more than kiss, but Stella had thought about him constantly. Her mind wandered at the worst times, vivid flashes of his body—and what he could do with it—derailing entire conversations.

Almost every night since he'd first touched her, she used the lingering feeling of his fingers to bring herself to climax. A feeling of need balled tight in her stomach no matter how often she orgasmed.

But while she was desperate to call him, she wanted to keep things professional until the contracts were signed.

It helped that she spent the last few nights moving into an Airbnb. Her lease was officially up. She put some things in storage but planned to buy mostly new for the house.

At the Airbnb, she was surrounded by unfamiliar furniture and knick-knacks. All she could hope was for Cal and his brothers to get the job done—fast.

To her surprise, when she arrived at the house, she was met with a team of guys. They weren't working yet, but were unpacking tools and machines.

Does Cal have guys?

She pulled up to the curb and took a deep breath, ready to face him with the no-nonsense focus of a client. Not his... whatever-the-hell-she-was.

"Hey!"

A knock at her passenger window made her jump. She put a hand to her chest as Travis waved through the glass.

"You're here!"

He hustled around the car and opened her door, offering a hand so she could step out. She'd purposefully worn pants and a sweater that covered her cleavage, not wanting to give Cal anything to look at but the contracts. She even had on bland black flats to complete the look.

"Don't worry," Travis said suddenly. "Nobody's started anything yet. We just wanted them here so we can get going as soon as. Since Cal said you're eager to get inside."

Stella nodded and followed him into the house. It looked the same, but for a table and chairs near the back. Cal and Jase sat with their backs to the door, reviewing something on a laptop.

"Hey guys, the boss's here," Travis joked, putting out his hand so Stella would go first.

When Cal turned around, his eyes darkened. She noticed his lip curl at one end as he glanced at her chest. They both stood and smiled, Jase offering his hand to shake. When she took Cal's, he squeezed and licked his bottom lip.

Fuck. This is gonna be hard.

He pulled out the seat beside him, and when she sat, Stella noticed she was a lot closer to him than the others. So close, their legs touched under the table.

"So, did you get a chance to go over everything?" Jase asked, breaking the silence.

"Um, yeah. It all looks great. I had a friend at work take a peek, and he's happy. So am I. Although..." She paused and reached for her copy, finding the highlighted page. "I was a little confused about this. It's like half of what Marco was charging," she said, pointing to the number given for labor costs.

Travis looked at Jase, who looked at Cal. He cleared his throat, and she felt his leg move away.

Uh oh.

"We know we're not an official company, and you're taking a chance on us. Most of those guys are friends and contractors we know. They've agreed to let us pay a lower rate in the hopes this job turns into more."

Stella searched his eyes, seeing nothing but her contractor.

"Okay. I mean, I guess that's your choice since they're your guys. But then...what about you? I don't see room in that budget for you three."

Jase took over. "Like Cal said, you're taking a chance on us. And so are we. We're not looking to make a profit out of this; we're looking to make a name for ourselves. And with a house like this, I think we can do that."

Being an accountant, Stella had never been uncomfortable talking about money. But what did make her uncomfortable was the idea that Cal and his brothers would be working for nothing and that their guys wouldn't get what they were worth.

"I've seen your work, and I know Cal's," she began, looking around the room before dropping her finger on the amount in question. "I'm not okay with that. At the very least, your guys deserve to get what they're worth. I want their best, after all. Why would they give that to me if they're underpaid?"

Cal shifted at her side, but it was Travis who spoke. "They'll give you their best, I can assure you—"

"Then they'll get paid for it."

Stella sat back and waited. She rested her hands openly on the table, inviting their response.

"Okay," Cal said eventually, his leg back against hers.

"Okay," she echoed, pushing back a little.

Other than that, the rest of the meeting was light and easy. The guys were eager to get started and happy to go along with anything and everything Stella wanted.

When she told them she was thinking about brushed brass in the kitchen, they agreed. When she said she wanted a skylight in the bathroom upstairs, they told her it would be costly but doable. And when she said she was hoping for an outdoor kitchen, their only request was to be the first to get a meal.

Done. Done. Double done.

By the time they were through, the guys were in full swing, hammering and drilling all around. Stella checked her watch and decided to order lunch for them all. Pizzas and sodas were always a hit.

While waiting for the food, she walked around with Jase and Travis, talking about the tiles, paint, and windows she hoped for. They were respectful but knowledgeable, giving her ideas and advice without making her feel like an asshole.

The food arrived within the hour, and the crew seemed thrilled by her small gesture. She met a handful of the guys, even speaking broken Spanish with a few. They liked that even more than the pizza.

When she finally grabbed a slice of her own, Cal appeared out of nowhere.

"You didn't have to do this, you know." He reached for a slice and took a big bite.

"I wanted to. I want these guys happy."

"And you didn't have to...you know. With the budget." Cal looked at his feet, embarrassed.

"It's not about" —Stella lowered her voice and checked to make sure nobody was close by— "you and me. It's about what's fair."

His face lit up, and he leaned into her ear. "You have no idea how badly I wanna fuck you right now."

Stella's pussy jolted awake, wishing he'd put his hands on her. But they were surrounded by people, including his brothers. Not the best time.

"Soon," she breathed.

At least, I hope.

The guys filtered in and out, and the pizzas soon vanished. Sensing it was time to leave them to it, she found Travis and Jase and said goodbye, telling them to call her if they had questions. She'd be back, of course, but she didn't want them to think she was hovering.

She didn't see Cal on her way out, and her heart dropped. She was hoping for one last look before rushing to work. As much as she wanted to wait, she'd only taken the morning off and had a meeting scheduled in the afternoon.

She was at the side of the house when he caught up with her. Almost the exact same spot he'd come to her that day she'd argued with Marco about the tiles.

"You gotta rush off so soon?" Cal called.

Stella glanced around, but none of the guys could see them from where they stood. They were all in front of or inside the house.

"I gotta work. This house won't pay for itself, ya know."

Cal took a step closer, his hand catching her fingers. "How long do you have?"

Her heart thumped in her ears, and she felt a pull in her core. "I have a meeting in two hours."

Cal put a hand on his chin and thought about it before whispering, "That should work."

Then he grabbed her hand and pulled.

twenty

. . .

"CAL!" Stella hissed as he dragged her past her car and towards a van. Her eyes bulged, and she glanced back, hoping none of the guys could see.

"No way."

No fucking way.

"Where's your sense of adventure?" he asked, smirking as he reached for the back handle.

It was a large moving van—roomy enough to make her nervous. When the door swung open, Stella coughed out a laugh when she spotted the mattress. It was covered in plastic and leaning against the side.

Cal hopped up and grasped the bag, tugging until it fell flat. Then he grabbed Stella's wrist and yanked her inside, his other hand slamming the door behind them.

"How long has this thing been in here?"

"It's brand new. Jase picked it up this morning, and he's taking it home later. In fact..."

He raised his eyebrows and took a few steps to the side, reaching into some boxes. He pulled a sheet out of nowhere, tore off the wrapper, and flicked it flat over the mattress.

"I don't know—"

"Shhh." He put a finger over her lips.

Taking her head in his hands, Cal pulled Stella into a kiss. A long, hot, needy kiss. His hands traced down her back as she wrapped her arms around his neck.

What is this guy doing to me?

She reached for his shirt and pulled, lifting it up and over his back until they had to break their kiss so it could fall free. Cal took the time to grab her sweater, yanking it up until he could see her bra.

"Why would you hide those?" he whispered, placing both hands under each breast, lifting them a little as he admired the red lace.

Before she could reply, he reached around and unhooked her bra. Catching it in one hand, he swooped in with his mouth, taking her right nipple so fast, she cried out.

Stella put her hand into his hair and groaned, reaching for his belt buckle.

"Uh-uh," Cal said suddenly, pushing himself back and raising the bra between them. "Hands."

Hands?

That one word sent a shock to her clit, and she immediately felt her pulse quicken.

"You trust me, right?"

Stella nodded and held out her hands. He wrapped the bra around her wrists, locking them together before he lifted them over her head, using the strap like a hook.

The angle brought her tits together, and he took the opportunity to bite at them, holding her close so she couldn't escape. Then he tucked her arms over his head until they fell around his neck. Using his now-free hands, he reached under her waistband and gently slipped her pants down.

Using his foot to get them off her feet, Cal grabbed her ass and lifted her up, at the same time stepping onto the mattress. He lowered them both until Stella's back touched the sheet, her arms still snug around his neck.

Cal touched her nose with his and kissed her quickly before ducking down, capturing her nipples in his lips and fingers. His right hand grasped her wrists and forced them back over her head.

He grinned—and to her surprise, looped her bra onto a small metal hook on the wall. She squirmed and glanced up. No doubt it was meant to hold down furniture. Now, it held her.

Uhhhh….

Part of her was instantly nervous. But mostly, she felt absolute lust knowing Cal was in complete control. He trailed his hands down her arms, drawing goosebumps on her flesh. When he rounded her breasts, he kissed them gently before falling down to her panties.

Dark Eyes looked up at her, his tongue flicking to meet her skin. Stella raised her hips, all but begging for him to touch her. Instead of giving her what she wanted, he reached up and released her hands, whispering, "On your knees."

Stella did as she was told, flipping over as fast as she could. Cal was quick, hooking the bra back in place so she was precisely how he wanted her.

"Feel okay?"

She nodded.

"Stay still."

He was at her side then, one hand lightly stroking her right ass cheek and the other pinching her nipples. He played her like a piano, and she wasn't sure how long she'd last without him inside.

At the angle, she had to lower her upper body, which made her ass stick up in the air. She felt his breath on her back as he came close and kissed her shoulder and neck. Then he put his hand over the fabric of her panties and pressed. He found her clit in one go, and she lurched forward, drawing a laugh from his lips. With his other hand still pinching her nipple, Cal rubbed along her warmth, putting pressure on her mound when he moved his hand low enough.

Stella started to move her hips, desperate for him to get rid of the panties. But he ignored her and kept up his torture, grabbing at the material and pulling it tight.

"Oh, fuck," Stella moaned as it grazed her clit.

When he spanked her, it was hard and fast, and she felt the heat inside building, wishing he would move his hand closer.

He did. The next slap was closer still, almost right on her core. She groaned and gasped, trying to keep her hands where he'd put them. Part of her wanted to stay quiet, afraid someone outside might hear. But somehow, she knew he wanted her to moan.

A hard tug on her nipple was met with another slap, only this time, he hit her right in the middle. Pain and pleasure swirled through her pussy, making her gasp for a breath.

She could feel warmth over her ass and smiled as he stroked her skin gently. Then he grabbed the material again. But instead of pulling it tight, he yanked it aside, and his tongue was on her.

"Oh my god. Fuck!" she screamed.

His tongue caressed her swollen lips before moving down, around and over her clit. When he pulled back, she felt his fingers replace his mouth. He pressed them into her and rubbed back and forth and up and down until she couldn't see straight.

When her breathing really became short, and her hips rolled uncontrollably, Cal shifted, and before she knew it, his cock was at her opening. He leaned around her waist and stroked her mound, at the same time pushing inside agonizingly slowly. He gave her every inch, bit by bit, until she was full.

Then he pulled back and drove inside, the sound of skin on skin filling the van. Stella grasped at the edge of the mattress as Cal pounded into her, his fingers somehow still on her clit.

She wanted to cum so badly, but she also wanted the pleasure to last as long as possible. She was acutely aware of how he filled her and shifted her hips so he could go even deeper.

She wanted to turn and face him. But all she could do was hold on and let him have his way with her.

Soon enough, she was whimpering and gasping for air.

Hearing how close she was, Cal pulled his hand away, reaching instead for her nipple, which he pulled at and twisted, not once slowing down his assault on her dripping wet pussy. His thick cock rammed into her over and over, and it was all she could do to stay on her knees.

Finally, he slowed, grasped her hips, and let out a rushed breath. She turned her head, and Cal pulled himself free the second they made eye contact. He shuffled up the mattress, unhooked her hands, and rolled her onto her side, nestling in behind, his chest to her back.

Stella lifted her leg, giving him better access as he slipped inside once more. At the new angle, she could just about reach around to kiss him. But when his fingers dragged against her clit, she dropped her head back.

"Oh god. Oh shit!"

Cal's hips kept up the pace, and soon, the rubbing on her mound turned into light taps, which got harder and faster the closer she got to climax.

When she came, Cal put his free hand over her mouth, the scream loud enough to be heard from outside the van. He groaned his own orgasm, grabbing at her breast as he pumped into her a few more times.

Spent, Stella didn't move. Couldn't move.

Cal rolled to the side and chuckled. "Fuck, Stells. I don't know how much longer I can keep this up."

You?

Still out of breath, Stella furrowed her brow. "What does that mean?"

She looked at Cal, and he smiled. "That every time I see you, I wanna bend you over the nearest surface. But I'm not twenty anymore—I don't recover like I used to."

She instantly relaxed and laughed. "You seem to be keeping up just fine."

"I'm serious. It's like I can't think straight. I can't be around you without wanting to rip your clothes off and get my fingers in your pussy. Seeing you like that." He pointed to her still-bound wrists and blew out a breath. "I almost came before I even got inside."

"Well, the feeling's mutual," she said. When he waved her off, she added, "Hey. If I told you how many times I've gotten off just with you in my head, even you would blush. I mean, shit. I'm not with you for more than a minute or two, and my pussy's practically calling your name. Sometimes just at the thought of you!"

Cal opened his dark eyes and looked up at her. "Really?"

Stella rolled on top and ground her dripping sex into his groin. She rested her still-bound hands on his shoulders as she spoke. "I've never wanted to fuck like that before. And I've never wanted to fuck so often before. It's all you, Cal."

"Well, shit. I mean, that's great."

Stella kissed him and sat up. Cal cupped her breasts and sat up to meet her. He kissed and licked around her nipples while Stella ran her nails down his back.

Underneath, she felt a twitch.

"You say you're not twenty, but that thing doesn't seem to have an off switch."

Cal moved his hips in response, stretching his neck to kiss her lips. Stella gently started to move, their juices making her slick and warm. After a few strokes, she could feel he was more than ready.

"Don't you have to work?"

Stella bit her lip as he reached between them. She raised her hips and fell onto his throbbing cock with a deep sigh.

"Eventually," she breathed, finding her rhythm.

Cal grabbed her nipple between his teeth, letting her take the lead this time.

twenty-one

· · ·

HER DAY HAD BEEN LONG, and it as only three. Between her most needy clients, new budgets, and a meeting with a man who insisted he wanted to turn all his assets into gold, Stella was more than ready to head home.

She was halfway through reconciling her last expense report of the day when her desk phone buzzed.

"Stella," her receptionist said, voice uncertain, "there's a Marco Silva here asking to see you. He says it's about your house?"

For a second, Stella couldn't breathe. Her pen paused mid-stroke, her fingers stiffening over the paper.

"Did he have an appointment?"

"No," the receptionist said. "But he said there's a problem."

She hadn't told anyone at the firm about her issues with Marco. Why would she?

"Put him in Conference B. I'll be right there."

Stella hung up and thought about calling for security. But her pride got the best of her. She stood slowly and reached for the navy blazer slung over the back of her chair. It was crisp and tailored and made her feel powerful.

And right now, she needed every ounce of that energy.

By the time she walked into the conference room, Marco was already positioned near the windows, sitting back in the chair like he belonged. He turned when he heard the door open and smiled warmly.

"Stella," he said, as if they were old friends reuniting. "Wow. Corporate really suits you."

She didn't smile back. "What are you doing here, Marco?"

"Easy," he said, holding his hands up like she'd pulled a gun. "Just wanted to talk. Clear the air."

"You could've emailed. Or called. Or not shown up at all."

"I figured this would be better. Face to face. You know, more... personal."

She folded her arms across her chest and sighed. "Say what you came to say."

He leaned onto the table and laid his hands out. "Look, I know things got heated. You were stressed, I was... maybe a little out of line. But come on. We had a good thing going. And now you've got what—some random guy and his brothers handling your build?"

Stella didn't answer.

Marco scoffed. "You really think they can finish that place? Cal used to haul drywall for me. That's it. He's not a builder. He's a laborer. And now he's in charge of *your* dream house?"

He said it like it was an insult. Like she was stupid for trusting someone else. Like *he* hadn't disrespected her in her own home.

"Are you finished?" she asked.

He blinked. "No. I'm offering you a second chance. I'll take the job back—start clean. We can pretend that little spat didn't happen."

The audacity nearly knocked her off her feet.

"You think I want you back on my project after what you said to me? After what you *did*?"

His smile dropped. "You're letting your ego get in the way of a smart decision."

"No," she said, her voice level. "I'm letting my *self-respect* get in the way of a bad one."

Marco's jaw tightened, and he narrowed his eyes. The smile was long gone now.

"You think those guys will get you across the finish line? You're dreaming. They don't have the connections. The vendors. The know-how. I built relationships in this town. You don't want to be blacklisted, Stella."

"Is that a threat?"

"It's a warning," he said darkly. "You burned a bridge with me. Be careful who else you piss off."

Stella stepped forward and leaned onto the table. "Get out, Marco. I don't want your advice. I don't want your help. I *don't want you*. If you show up here or at my house again, I'll have you removed."

The big man jutted his jaw, then stood and ambled to the door.

"Bitch," he muttered under his breath.

She didn't flinch. "Don't make me slap you again."

He held her gaze for one more second before turning and leaving with stiff shoulders and clenched fists. The door slammed shut behind and Stella stood there for a moment, heart pounding, heat rising to her cheeks. She walked slowly to the window and watched as he crossed the parking lot, his gait tense, head down.

Her phone was already in her hand before she realized what she was doing. She pulled up Cal's number. Her thumb hovered over the call button.

He'd come running. He'd be angry. Protective. He might even offer to knock Marco's teeth in. And part of her wanted that.

But another part of her—the part that had calmly thrown Marco out of her office—knew better.

What would that help?

She could handle Marco.

twenty-two

. . .

BY THE TIME Stella reached her Airbnb, her nerves were frayed and her head was pounding. Marco's smug little scene at the office had left her simmering. All she wanted now was a hot shower, a glass of wine, and possibly a frozen pizza she could burn in peace.

She fished the key out of her bag, slipped it into the lock, opened the door, and froze.

Todd was sitting on the couch like it belonged to him. Like *she* still belonged to him. His elbows rested on his knees, hoodie pulled over his head. His sneakers were kicked off, one foot tapping anxiously on the floor, like he'd been there a while.

You've got to be kidding me.

"Hey," he said, as if this was normal. As if it were any other night.

Stella didn't move. Her keys clinked as her hand tightened around them.

"What are you doing here? How did you get in?"

He stood, brushing his palms down his jeans. "The landlady gave me a key."

"Why... what...?"

He smiled sheepishly. "I'm still on your account, remember? I just emailed and told her I needed to grab something, but forgot the keys. She let me in."

Stella's jaw clenched. "So you lied."

He shrugged, already defensive. "I just needed to talk to you."

"I told you we were done."

"Yeah, well, people say shit when they're angry."

Stella dropped her bag on the counter with a thud. "I wasn't angry. I was *done.* There's a difference."

Todd stepped closer, condescension in his voice. "Stells, come on. I know you're stressed. The house, work, all of it—it's a lot. You've been through a rough few weeks, and I get it. But that doesn't mean you throw everything away."

She laughed. "You really think I walked away because of a *rough few weeks*?"

He blinked, surprised by her tone.

"I walked away because I finally opened my fucking eyes, Todd. You haven't been my partner in a long time. You've been a burden. One I let stay because I felt *guilty.*"

That struck something. His posture shifted, his mouth flattening into a hard line.

"I was there for you when no one else was," he said quietly. "When your sister died, I didn't leave. I held you together. You think any of your other boyfriends would've done that?"

She flinched. Just slightly. But he saw it.

"And now what? You meet a flannel-wearing handyman with muscles, and you're suddenly over it? Over *me*?"

Stella took a breath and pursed her lips. "You're right," she said softly. "You were there. When I fell apart, when I couldn't even *breathe*, you helped me. You sat with me. You took care of me. And I will *always* be grateful for that."

Todd's face softened, as if he thought she was coming around.

"But that was two years ago," she added.

His brow creased.

"You helped me through the worst time in my life," she said. "But that doesn't give you a pass to check out of our relationship.

To mooch off me. To treat me like an ATM with benefits while you played video games all day and called it ambition."

He opened his mouth, but she steamrolled ahead.

"You stopped trying. You stopped being kind. You stopped being present. And then you acted like *I* was the problem. You let me feel broken for months because you didn't want to admit you were the one who changed."

"I didn't—"

"You did," she snapped. "You stopped seeing me as a partner and started seeing me as a safety net. And I'm done being that for you."

Todd's chest rose and fell with frustration. "You don't mean that."

"I *do.*"

He stepped forward again, voice rising. "You really think you're gonna get that house finished without me and Marco?"

Her stomach twisted. *Marco?*

"You're not the only one he talked to, Stella. He came to me, too."

Her face tightened. "What are you talking about?"

Todd smirked. "He said he can forgive you. We both can."

"Forgive me?" Stella shook her head, incredulous. "You two deserve each other."

"Oh, come on." He ran a hand through his hair. "We were *good* together. You know we were. You just got in your head and started treating me like some loser—"

"You *became* one!" she snapped. "I didn't make you stop showering. I didn't make you quit job hunting. You gave up, Todd! And you thought you could coast forever."

"You were supposed to be on my side," he shouted.

"And you were supposed to be on *mine.*" Her voice cracked, emotion pushing its way out. "But I needed a partner, not a shadow. I needed someone who saw me, not someone who resented me the second I started outgrowing him."

Todd stared at her, nostrils flaring. "So that's it? We're just over?"

"We've *been* over. You just didn't want to see it."

He stepped back like she'd slapped her. "I loved you," he said.

"I believe that you did once. But I stopped loving you a long time ago."

Todd didn't speak. He just stood there for a long, heavy beat before nodding once and heading toward the door.

He grasped the handle and whispered, "Don't come crawling back when he turns out to be a mistake."

"I won't," she said, voice clear and steady. "Not to you."

He left without another word. Stella stood there for a moment, hands braced on the kitchen counter, her pulse hammering in her throat.

Again, she wanted to call Cal. To tell him what happened. Let him soothe the ache.

But what would that change?

Todd was done. Marco, too.

And while Cal meant something—was *starting* to mean something—this was a fight Stella had to win on her own.

She opened the fridge, poured a glass of wine, and sat on the edge of the couch.

Tomorrow, she'd go back to the site.

Tomorrow, she'd face the crew and finish what she started.

Tonight, she raised her glass in a quiet toast to her own goddamn strength.

twenty-three

. . .

one week later

"UM, excuse me, bitch—what the fuck?"

Stella grinned, Jenny's face a mix of shock and awe.

"What?" she asked with a knowing smirk.

Jenny lifted her hand and circled her finger in the air, gesturing for Stella to spin around and show off her outfit. She was wearing black high heels with sexy stockings and a very short black skirt. If she sat and crossed her legs, Jenny would get a glimpse of the garter around her thigh.

On top, she chose a simple white shirt, but underneath, she had on a leather corset that held her tits so high she could almost rest her chin on them.

Too much?

"Biiiiiitch," Jenny exclaimed, clapping her hands in excitement. "Tell me you're fucking that guy?"

Biting her lip, Stella nodded, and the pair clasped hands in excitement. The hostess had to clear her throat to get their attention.

"Your table's ready," she announced with zero enthusiasm.

Sure enough, when Stella sat, Jenny got a good look at the

garter belt. She even leaned over and tugged the skirt higher, not totally sure what she was seeing.

"You're like, my fucking idol. Seriously. You look ridiculously sexy. And…happy."

With a slight nod, Stella grinned. "I am. And I'm sorry I've been so absent. It's just been insane and—"

"Oh, girl. I. Do. Not. Care. Whatever the fuck is making you look like this" —she wagged her finger up and down, her eyes drawn to the cleavage— "needs to stay. Fuck, where can I get some?"

The waiter took their order, and Stella talked about the progress of the house and how amazing the new crew was. But when their food arrived, Jenny put up her hand.

"Okay. I've been good. I've sat and listened and smiled and nodded. Now it's time to dish. Tell me about his cock. *Please*. In excruciating detail. I wanna know exactly what he does with that thing so I can tell the morons I've been dating how to up their fucking games."

Stella blew out a breath and thought about how much to share. The truth was, she'd never been that open, and though she was excited about Cal, she wasn't sure she wanted Jenny to know *everything*.

But then, she was dying to spill, too.

Fuck it.

"Okay. Um, I guess it started the day I dumped Todd. Like literally minutes after that. He came in—"

"Hold up," Jenny said suddenly, her hand in the air. "*The day you dumped Todd*. As in, before we met for coffee?"

Stella bit her lip. "Kinda. I'm sorry, I just didn't know what it was and—"

Jenny lifted her other hand and looked off to the side. Then she nodded, took a breath, and smiled. "I'm over it. Continue."

"And that's why I love you." Stella took a sip of water and gathered her thoughts. "Okay. So…um…right. So, Todd and everyone left, and he stayed back. I was all upset, but he came to see if I was okay. And we just…" She looked around and lowered her voice. "Fucked, right there and then!"

Jenny speared a piece of chicken and sat with her mouth open, eyes wide.

"And then he tells me he can help me finish the house. And then we fucked *again*. Then, right before I met his brothers—"

"If you fucked a trio of sexy construction guys, I'm gonna lose my goddamn mind."

Shit. I wish.

"I mean, they're pretty fucking sexy. And if I'm being honest, I think Jase has been flirting. They don't know about me and Cal, so…"

Stella took a bite and thought about her last encounter with Jase. After she and Cal left the van, she ran into Jase by her car. He was smoking and talking on the phone. When he saw her, he hung up and smiled. He didn't try anything or say anything flirty, but she could see something in his eyes. And the way he held the door open for her to get in the car was a little too close.

"So forget the brothers. This Cal fucked you in the house. How many times?"

"Uh," Stella began, but Jenny reached over and smacked her hand.

"Are you fucking counting right now? If you have to count, it's more than two."

Stella bit her lip again. "It's definitely more than two. After that first night, I went back the next day to meet his brothers and talk about the house. And before I know it, he's…" —she mouthed the word 'fucking' as the waiter walked by— "me on the rickety table in the kitchen. Like, really fucking. And… I don't know. It's like we just can't keep our hands off each other. Then when I went by to finish the contracts and meet the new crew, we wound up fucking in a moving van."

"Please tell me he goes down on you and doesn't just—"

"Jen, I swear to god. I've never been with a guy so into me. He will do everything in his power to hear me moan, and he, like, refuses to cum first. Like he has to make me cum before he'll orgasm."

Jenny put her fork down and fanned herself with the napkin. "Fuck, Stells. This guy sounds too good to be true. I almost wish he had a small dick."

Not a chance.

"Sorry."

"I hate you, you know? Just a little, but I fucking hate you."

They both smiled and laughed. Stella was happy her friend finally knew everything. Lying about Cal had been tough.

Eventually, she managed to turn the conversation away from Cal and asked about Jenny and her work. But just as she started telling a story about her new boss, Stella heard her phone chime. Worried it could be work, she reached in and opened it up without really thinking.

She tried her best to keep her expression neutral, even with Cal, naked and hard, front and center on the screen. Gulping down a breath, she locked the phone quickly and stuffed it back in her bag.

She tried to focus on her friend, but he'd already lit the match.

Like he knew it would.

When Jenny took a breath, Stella excused herself, rushing to the bathroom and into a stall. She sat and opened the phone again to see what he'd sent.

I need to fuck you today

In the picture, he was in her upstairs bathroom, his abs tense and his dick long and hard. She licked her lips and felt her pussy clench. She'd never sent a nude before, and she was hesitant to start now. But she just couldn't help herself.

Just keep your face out of it.

As quickly as she could, she took off her jacket and unbuttoned her shirt. It fell open to reveal the leather corset, which she'd bought for Cal. The front had a hook under her boobs, which kept them steady but plump. She undid the snap and pulled the left side down, angling the phone to get some of the leather and a little of her neck.

Her nipple was already hard, but she licked her finger and ran it over the top to make it glisten. Then she took the snap and sent it off before she could stop herself.

Cal replied in seconds.

> When can you get over here?

The message came with another attachment, only this time it was a short video. He was sitting now, his thick cock in his big hands, stroking slowly up and down.

Stella clenched again and found a sudden urge to be bad. She sent Jenny a quick text.

> BRB. Work call

After that, she opened the FaceTime app. Then she hesitated. *Don't be a pussy. Just do it.*

Before she hit Cal's contact, she shuffled out of her panties, lining up the shot so, again, her face wouldn't show. But he'd get a full glimpse of the stockings and garter.

Though she didn't need to, Stella licked her fingers. Then she tapped the little green phone icon and started to masturbate. Cal's face filled the screen, complete shock and lust in his eyes. He sat mouth open as she ran her fingers up and down her glistening pussy, showing him exactly how wet she was. Then she rounded her clit, just as he got his dick back out.

Neither said a word, but heavy breathing filled the mercifully empty bathroom. She watched him pleasure himself, his white knuckles jerking up and down as fast as he could manage. She matched his pace, rubbing her clit until she had no choice but to cry out.

Cal came a few seconds later, groaning from the screen as he squirted his seed on his leg. They both sat, breathless and semi-satisfied, but Stella ended the call before he could say anything.

Let him think about that for the rest of the day.

Carefully, she cleaned herself up and got dressed. Then she washed up and went back out to Jenny.

"All good?"

"Sorry," Stella said. "It was nothing. Just a silly question about a budget."

"You sure. You're all red."

Stella pressed the back of her hand to her cheek. "Oh, yeah. This new temp is a moron. He needs me to hold his hand through everything. I just get frustrated when I have to repeat myself, is all."

Jenny shrugged and went back to her food. Stella tried, but in her head, she was already on her knees

twenty-four

· · ·

AFTER A LONG LUNCH, Stella went back to the office. As much as she wanted to swing by the house, she had a deadline she couldn't ignore. So, she closed the door, turned off her phone, and put on her headphones.

Music cranked, she tried to focus—but her mind kept slipping.

No matter how hard she worked, her thoughts wandered back to Cal. To the way his voice had dipped low during their call. To the way he watched her—like he could eat her alive and make it last.

By the time she finally wrapped up, the sky outside was dark, and her stomach was growling. She'd nearly forgotten she was still in her sexiest outfit—leather corset, garters, and all.

What a waste.

She drove home, forgetting her phone was off until she pulled into the driveway. When she turned it on, it buzzed with two messages and a missed call.

> You're fucking unreal. But I wanna see that in person

> Do you think you'll make it by tonight?

She winced.

She'd wanted to. God, she wanted to. But now it was late.

> Hey, sorry. I just got home. I had to get a bunch of stuff done

> Maybe tomorrow?

She parked, gathered her things, and hustled inside—more than ready to strip down and crawl into bed. But when she rounded the corner, she stopped short.

Cal was there. Sitting casually against the door, ankles crossed, a bag of takeout at his side.

"Cal?"

"Hey, you." He stood, crossed the hall in two strides, and wrapped his arms around her. The kiss was deep, immediate. Familiar. As if it had been hours, not days.

"Have you been waiting long?" she asked, a twinge of guilt settling low in her stomach.

"Not long. I figured you were busy, but... I wanted to see you." He lifted the takeout bag. "And I brought sushi."

Stella softened, reaching for his hand. "You didn't have to do that."

"I wanted to."

They stepped inside. Stella tossed her bag onto the counter while Cal opened the fridge. He slid the sushi in and turned, stepping into her space again.

This time, he didn't kiss her right away. He just looked.

"What?" she asked.

His voice was low. "That outfit's been on my mind all day."

Her stomach flipped. "I thought about stopping by..."

He leaned in. "So did I. I almost drove to your office and told everyone to leave."

Stella laughed, already leaning toward him. "I considered doing the same at the house."

"I knew you were dangerous."

"I knew you were trouble."

His lips brushed hers, but he didn't deepen the kiss. Not yet. Instead, he cradled her jaw with one hand and slipped the other beneath her shirt, his thumb tracing the edge of the corset.

"You wore this for me," he murmured.

"I didn't say that."

"No, but I can feel it."

Her pulse quickened. He was warm and solid and already hard. But instead of rushing, he just held her. One hand at her waist, the other on the back of her neck.

"I missed you," he said quietly.

"I missed you, too."

He exhaled, like that confession had been sitting heavy on his chest. His lips brushed her cheek, then her jaw, then her neck.

"I thought about our call," she whispered.

He chuckled against her skin. "Yeah? I've been hard since noon."

Stella turned her face and kissed him slowly. "I don't need anything wild tonight," she murmured. "Just you."

He nodded, his eyes soft. "You've got me."

She reached for his hand and led him toward the bedroom.

It was slow. Tender. The kind of night where breathing together felt like foreplay, and touch came before need. He was gentle, even though she could feel how badly he wanted to lose control.

When it was over, Stella lay there in the quiet, her body humming, her legs like jelly, her sex deliciously sore.

She'd never had a man like Cal. Or rather, never *been had* by a man like Cal. He knew exactly what he wanted—and somehow, exactly what she needed. He read her body like it was his own, touching her gently when she needed it, and not-so-gently when she *really* needed it.

Fuck. I'm done for.

She smiled and kissed him, her hands cupping his cheeks as a wave of affection rolled through her. He gently let go of her leg and pulled her close, deepening the kiss.

Eventually, he pulled back and gave her a sheepish look. "Sorry. I just couldn't wait."

She smirked and winced a little as he shifted beside her. He looked around the room, then back to her, suddenly unsure of what to do next.

"Maybe a shower?" she offered.

They went in together, kissing and caressing under the hot spray. When it came time to clean herself, Stella stood to one side, hesitating.

Cal noticed immediately. "You okay?"

"Yeah, sorry. I just… I can wait—"

"What?"

She waved him off and looked away. "It's fine. I can wait until you're done."

He blinked. "Wait? For what?"

"Well, I mean… Todd didn't, uh, like it when I—"

His expression twisted.

"That little fuck nugget got weird about you cleaning your pussy?"

She nodded, embarrassed. "He didn't want to see the cum. Or something."

"He didn't wanna see *his own* cum? His *fucking jizz*?"

Cal shook his head and grabbed the soap. He adjusted the showerhead and stepped in close, kissing her collarbone.

She gasped softly as the cool water hit her thighs.

"That little asshole didn't deserve to be near this thing, let alone *in* it," he muttered, nudging her leg open to rinse her gently. "He should've been on his knees licking you clean."

Stella's breath caught as he carefully soaped her, his fingers slow and sure. He washed her gently, avoiding the clit with practiced grace, then ran the water down her stomach to rinse her off.

She closed her eyes, overwhelmed by him.

"How could anyone be this close and not want to touch you?" he murmured, dragging his fingers along her stomach.

As if on cue, it growled.

Cal grinned. "Okay, okay. Dinner it is."

twenty-five

· · ·

AFTER THE SHOWER, when they were both dressed and spent, Cal grabbed the bag of sushi from the fridge.

"Wanna find a movie?" Stella asked, grabbing the remote.

"Sure."

Perched on the edge of the couch, Stella clicked on the TV and scrolled through the endless list of titles. Cal hummed to himself in the kitchen as he plated the food and opened a couple of beers.

"Hope you're hungry," he said with a laugh, joining her on the couch. "I got way too much."

Stella's eyes widened, but her stomach growled at the sight of it all.

"I think we'll manage."

She left the remote on the coffee table, hoping he'd take the lead. He did, scrolling for a few minutes before settling on an episode of *Friends*.

"We don't have to," Stella said quickly, trying to downplay the fact that her watch count was in the triple digits.

But Cal just waved his chopsticks. "I love this show."

After sushi and a few episodes, Cal yawned and stood, stretching as he reached for his jacket.

Stella narrowed her eyes, a knowing smirk forming. "It's kinda late. You really gonna drive all the way home?"

He grinned. "I didn't want to assume."

It felt natural to ask him to stay. But once they were in bed, a flicker of anxiety crept in. They'd had sex more times than she could count—but it had always been wild, lusty, desperate sex. Not soft. Not quiet. Not the kind of sex that usually involved… cuddling.

Until now.

So when he slipped under the covers beside her, she wasn't sure what to expect.

Do we spoon? A crisp high-five?

To her surprise, he shuffled closer, grabbed her arm, and pulled her back against him. He slotted in behind her, warm and solid, wrapping an arm around her waist. He kissed her shoulder and sighed—fast asleep within minutes.

When Stella woke the next morning, they were still tangled together. His arm rested on her hip, and she could feel the warmth of his breath on her neck. She turned slightly to look, and he instinctively pulled her closer, his head finding her pillow.

The clock read 6:48 a.m., and she knew she had to be up soon. But she couldn't bring herself to break the moment. So she closed her eyes again and let herself sink into it.

The next time she woke, it was 7:34. The sudden cold at her back told her Cal had moved, and a second later, she heard the bathroom door close quietly.

Just be cool. Don't make it weird, and it won't be weird.

Stella got up, threw on a sweater, and padded to the kitchen, her eyes half-closed. She started the coffee, popped a bagel in the toaster, and grabbed a couple of plates.

"Mornin'," Cal said from behind her.

He stood at the bedroom door, his hair messy, a sleepy smile on his face. "Is that coffee?"

She nodded and gestured toward the counter. "I got bagels, too. You like 'em toasted, or…"

"Toasted. Sure."

He wandered her way, yawning as he placed a hand on her lower back and pressed a quick kiss to her cheek—more polite than passionate.

When the bagel popped, he took it and asked, "You?"

Stella nodded again and offered a small smile.

He dropped another bagel into the toaster, then added cream cheese and smoked salmon to his. Stella poured the coffee, placing his cup by his plate before retrieving the milk and sugar.

They sat on the couch, Cal flipping to the weather channel as they ate in comfortable silence—until it wasn't so comfortable anymore.

The bagel disappeared fast. But he still hadn't said much.

Uh-oh.

Stella finished her food and wrapped both hands around her mug. She tucked her legs under her and took a long sip, savoring the warmth. When she opened her eyes, Cal was looking her way with a half smile.

"Last night was great," he said.

But…

"But I should get going. The guys'll already be at the site, and if this forecast's right," he jerked a thumb at the screen, "we gotta get that skylight in before the rain hits."

"Right," Stella said, trying to read his tone.

Cal stood and grabbed their plates, placing them in the dishwasher before disappearing into the bedroom. When he came back, he was fully dressed—shoes on, keys in hand.

"You okay?" he asked, shrugging on his jacket.

"Hmm? Oh yeah. Just thinking about work. I've got a few things to knock out this morning."

He nodded and turned toward the door.

Stella bit her cheek. "Are *you* okay?"

Cal turned back, brow furrowed. "Yeah, why?"

"You just seem a little… distant?" she said softly, eyes on her coffee.

He closed his eyes and rubbed his brow. "Shit. I'm sorry. I'm just not a morning person. I didn't mean to be a dick—I just don't really function before eight."

Stella let out a breath. His face softened again.

"Okay. Sorry. I just wanted to make sure." She blushed. "Go! You don't wanna be late."

He was halfway to the door when he suddenly spun around, like he'd just remembered something.

He dropped his keys on the table and crossed the room in a few quick steps, sinking into the couch in front of her. His hand found her face, and he kissed her hard—all tongue, teeth, and hands. He tasted like toothpaste and coffee, and she melted into him instantly.

His hand slipped beneath her sweater, gently cupping her breast. He teased her nipple with slow, confident fingers, then pulled back with a smirk.

"See you later?"

"Definitely."

He left with a bounce in his step. Stella sat back, biting her lip.

Is this too good to be true?

"Hey, Cal?" she called before he reached the door. "I have this work thing coming up. It's no big deal, but it's a couple nights away. By the beach."

Cal tilted his head. "Okay. I mean, we can still be in touch if we have—"

"No," she said quickly. Then, catching herself: "I mean, yes, we can talk. But that's not why I'm telling you. I was, uh… wondering if you'd want to come with me. A couple nights away."

His grin spread wide. "A couple nights away. With you? By the beach? Count me in."

"You sure you can get away? What would your brothers think?"

His smile faltered. He came back to the couch and sat, elbows on his knees.

"Actually… I was thinking maybe it's time we told them about us." He kept his eyes down, like he was afraid he'd crossed a line.

Stella's back went straight. "R—really? You think that's a good idea?"

"I get why you didn't want them to know at first. I really do. But this isn't just… fucking anymore. At least, not for me. And they're not going to lose respect for you because we're… whatever this is."

Not just fucking anymore?

Stella shifted in place, heart thudding. He was right. Travis and Jase wouldn't treat her differently. She *knew* that.

But still… what if they did?

After Marco, the last thing she wanted was a crew of guys second-guessing her every move.

"Just think about it?" Cal asked, his tone gentle.

"Yeah. I will."

He kissed her again, then finally made it out the door, leaving Stella alone with her thoughts.

If we tell them, then this is the real deal. Cal and me are… like, a couple.

But what if that changes things? What if he loses interest the second it's not sneaking around anymore?

The trip wasn't for another month or so. She had time to decide if she wanted to step out of the relationship closet—and to figure out whether Cal was really in it for the long haul.

Or if they'd crash and burn the moment things got too *normal*.

twenty-six

. . .

one month later

"HELLO?"

Stella snatched her purse and the client file from the passenger seat, juggling the phone between her ear and shoulder. She'd already spilled coffee on her shirt and was running late. A flawless start to her overbooked day.

"Hey, it's me," Cal said, ignoring her sharp greeting. "Just wanted you to know that the tiles should all be done by end of day. So if you wanna come by and see, then maybe we can figure out the fixtures finally?"

His voice calmed her instantly. She stopped rushing and took a deep breath, annoyed with herself for her tone.

Taking a cue from him, she chuckled. "I'm not gonna apologize for being particular. It's my house, right? I want what I want."

"Damn right," he said, letting out an amused breath. "Later?"

"Later."

Things had been amazing with Cal over the last month, and even better with the house. He and his brothers were ahead of schedule, and the place was coming along better than she'd hoped.

Marco had said he'd be done in six months, but Cal, Jase, and Travis were on track for five.

And even though he technically worked for her, Cal never made it weird between them. When he was on the job, he was her contractor. And when he wasn't, he was something else altogether.

Stella took another deep breath before pressing the elevator button. She used the final two minutes alone to organize her thoughts.

Jackson first. The Miller briefing second. Worry about Ms. Kim later.

Her firm had always been successful, and the partners were somewhat selective about their clients. But since Ms. Kim came on the scene, they'd taken on a number of her friends and business associates.

Stella had never had so much work. Which was great for her wallet. Just not for her mental health.

Of course, not worrying about a man-child at home made her life a lot easier. And she didn't even mind the Airbnb anymore.

I just have to swallow my pride and ask for an assistant.

It had been on her mind for a few weeks, and she knew they'd agree. It just stung her pride that she needed help. But with a new client coming in that day—someone big—Stella had made up her mind.

Her job was to review her clients' accounts to see what she could do to make rich people richer. At her firm, they guaranteed the best. That meant safe and secure with just the right amount of risk and high returns.

She didn't handle the markets and sales but was there to advise. Stella saw where a client could take risks and made suggestions, which often wound up being property. It was always a safe bet, no matter the climate.

Though landing this new client would mean a huge bonus, it also meant she hadn't seen Cal in almost a week. They'd called and FaceTimed, but it wasn't the same, and part of her was worried he was losing interest.

His texts had slowed, and they hadn't sexted in the last few days. But more than that, she missed him.

So, she made a point of leaving early to go see the tiles—and her man.

When Stella pulled up, the place was crowded with guys, so much so, she had to park on the next street. They were laying the driveway soon and had a lot of work to do to get the area ready.

Luckily, the street was big, with just a few houses, so they weren't in anyone's way. Even so, she made a mental note to bake her new neighbors cookies as a thank you.

Picking her way around the tools and equipment, Stella soon found herself face to face with the new front door. The last one they'd installed didn't fit right, and Jase had insisted they change it. And looking at the new one, she knew he'd been right.

Just as she reached for the handle, it opened in a rush, revealing Jase in all his toned and tanned glory.

"Stella, hey. Here to see the shower?" he asked, a knowing smile on his face.

"I'll say the same thing to you: I want what I want. And those fixtures were hideous!"

They both laughed, and he jerked his thumb over his shoulder, gesturing with his head to let her know to head upstairs.

He stepped to the side so she could pass. As she moved, she smelled an intoxicating mix of cologne and sweat. Without thinking, she glanced up and almost tripped when he locked his dark eyes on hers.

Fuck me, he's so much like Cal.

They hadn't come out of the relationship closet yet, and Stella knew Cal was getting anxious. He'd given her a week after the first mention and casually dropped the hint one Saturday morning over breakfast.

"If they knew about us, we could drive over there together," he'd said, lacing his fingers in hers.

But something was holding her back. Something she couldn't put her finger on. And it was only a matter of time before Cal called her on it.

Stella smiled at a couple of guys and ascended the stairs. The new banister looked great, and when she reached the top step, her master suite took her breath away.

The wall on the end was painted dark blue, and the skylight was in place. It looked huge without the furniture, and she couldn't wait to get everything inside.

She heard voices to her right and walked to the closet area, which was way bigger than she needed. That led to the master bathroom, which was at the front of the house, over the guest room. The new window sat snugly in the frame, and another skylight was in the center of the room.

Cal stood in the corner, scratching the stubble on his chin as one of his guys explained something technical. He had a clipboard in his other hand and a confused look on his face. He looked tired and very sexy.

She thought about those dark eyes for days, and now that he was so close, she had to hold herself back. But instead of jumping him, Stella wandered to the window and looked out over the street.

She didn't hear the guy leave or Cal move in behind.

His left hand cupped her ass, and his right lifted the hair from her neck, pulling it a little so she tilted her head. Kissing along her shoulders, Cal trailed his hand around to her stomach, running his fingers along the waist of her pants.

So much for him losing interest.

"Hey," Cal whispered before licking at her lobe. "What do you think?"

Stella let her head fall back, twisting until her lips met his. He kissed her, his tongue gently licking across her lip. He tasted like chocolate.

"It's incredible," she breathed when he finally let her go.

Moving to the middle of the room, Stella lifted her arms out and spun around, her eyes on the skylight and the blue sky above. When she stopped, Cal grabbed her hand and pulled her close.

"I meant the shower," he said, scooping her up and over his shoulder.

She let out a small yelp and then clapped a hand over her mouth.

"Cal!" she hissed, throwing a quick, nervous glance at the door.

When her feet touched the ground, she pursed her lips and put her hands on her hips. But the tile melted her fake anger like he knew it would. She ran her hand along the cold wall, loving the deep greens and tiny flecks of bronze.

The tile really did look amazing—but her focus had shifted. Entirely.

Cal stood at her back, his chest touching her shoulder. She could see in his eyes that he was just as horny as she was. The way he licked his lips made her clit stand to attention, and she bit her own lip in response.

The guys are right outside. This is a bad idea.

Taking the unspoken challenge, Cal ducked and wrapped his arms around her waist, pulling her into a kiss that caught her breath. His tongue swirled in her mouth as he pressed her into the wall.

Stella wound her arms around his neck and jumped, wrapping her legs around his waist as the kiss deepened. When his hands shifted, she squeezed tighter, locking herself in place.

Cal growled in response and grasped her hands together, lifting them over her head. He used one big hand to hold them both in place and tore at her shirt with his other until—

"You in here, Stella?" Travis called from the stairs.

Cal gently set her down and stepped back just in time, reining himself in as Jase entered like nothing had happened

"There you are." He glanced from Cal to Stella without so much as a raised eyebrow.

Jase smiled, his eyes lingering on Stella before he handed his brother a clipboard. "Signature, please."

Cal skimmed the paper and scrawled his name on the bottom before turning to the shower and announcing, "The Queen approves, boys. We're not fired."

Stella rolled her eyes and laughed, knowing full well they meant it in good fun. Travis eagerly moved in, showing her samples of the fixtures and the sleek, matching faucets. Jase and Cal murmured in the corner before one of their guys came in.

"Boss? The guy's here with the lumber for the deck."

"Oh, yeah? Great timing." Travis turned to Stella. "Wanna see the materials for the deck and outdoor kitchen?"

Her eyes lit up, and she nodded enthusiastically. The group left the bathroom and hurried down the stairs, crossing through the house to the huge double doors that led to the backyard and what was soon to be a big, beautiful deck.

The wood looked terrific, and she could see they'd already mapped out the area. They would build an outdoor kitchen to the right of the house with a blacktop grill and a green egg smoker. She was even splurging on refrigerators under the countertops.

Stella flipped through the samples, letting the guys talk specs in the background.

After a few minutes, she felt her phone buzz.

"Hey," she sang, happy to see Jenny's contact pop up on the screen.

"Stell?"

Stella's heart stopped. The blood drained from her face as the next sound came—a loud bang, followed by a crash that rattled down the line.

"Jenny?"

"Stella, I need you."

twenty-seven

. . .

"STELLA? THAT GUY—" Jenny's voice cracked, breathless with sobs.

A male voice thundered in the background, furious and unhinged. Stella couldn't make out the words, but it sounded like he was yelling to be let in—screaming at her.

"Jenny," Stella snapped, clutching her phone tighter. "Lock the fucking door and call the cops. I'm on my way."

She turned to find Cal and Jase already behind her, their expressions hard and concerned.

"It's Jenny," she said quickly, adrenaline spiking. "I think someone's breaking in. I don't know for sure, but she's terrified. I have to get there."

They didn't hesitate.

"Trav!" Jase shouted, already pulling Stella toward the house. "We gotta go. Now, bro!"

Cal moved in close, whispering something urgent to Travis and the delivery guy. Both looked up, confused but alarmed. Travis nodded, giving a quick wave toward the lumber, as if to say he'd take it from here.

Next thing Stella knew, she was in Cal's truck. Jase and Travis jumped in the back, and they peeled out of the unfinished driveway with a roar of tires.

"Call her," Cal ordered, his knuckles white on the steering wheel.

Stella hit Jenny's contact, praying she would answer. It rang once. Twice. Then—

"Stella? Oh my God, Stella, please—" Jenny's voice dissolved into broken sobs.

"I'm here," Stella said, tapping the button for the speaker. "Where are you right now?"

"I'm in the bathroom. I locked the door."

"Good. Did you call the cops?"

"I think so. I—I pressed the thing on my phone. I don't know. He just started pounding on the door and—oh God, Stell, I'm so scared."

"I know, I know. Just stay with me, okay? I'm minutes away. I can practically see your building."

There was silence on the line, aside from Jenny's shallow, ragged breathing.

"Jenny?"

"He's… he's still here…" she whispered.

Then the line went dead.

"Shit!" Stella gasped.

Cal looked over just long enough to catch her fear before slamming his foot harder on the gas.

Jenny's apartment was ten minutes away—fifteen with traffic.

They made it in five.

"What number?" Jase asked as they screeched into the parking lot.

"Fourteen! First floor on the right!"

Jase and Travis were out before the truck stopped moving. Stella followed, but they were already ahead, barreling into the courtyard with fists clenched and fury in their eyes.

By the time she caught up, the door to Jenny's apartment was smashed open.

Inside, chaos.

Furniture splintered. Glass everywhere. Yelling. The thud of fists hitting flesh.

Stella hovered at the entrance, frozen, until her eyes locked on the scene.

Travis stood over a man curled on the floor, his face already a mess of blood. Jase had him pinned with a knee to the ribs and one arm twisted back.

"Where's Jenny?" she asked, heart hammering.

"I got her!" Cal called from deeper in the apartment.

Stella followed his voice to the bathroom, where Jenny was crumpled in the corner, clinging to Cal with trembling hands. She looked so small, so wrecked. Her lip was split, and her cheeks were streaked with tears and blood.

"Is she—did he—?" Stella asked, then choked on the words.

The sight of her strongest, boldest friend reduced to this—it shattered something inside her.

Something primal took its place.

Stella turned and stormed back into the living room. The guy on the floor turned his head just in time to see her coming—right before her fist cracked into his face.

He groaned and tried to turn away. She hit him again. Hard.

Something cracked.

"Stella!" someone shouted.

But she couldn't stop. She hit him over and over until her fists ached.

Jase lunged, wrapping an arm around her waist to haul her off. Her foot lashed out, connecting with the guy's throat. He gurgled, clutching at his neck, gasping for air.

Sirens screamed down the street.

Police stormed in.

"Hands where we can see them!" an officer barked.

But Stella kept going. Her elbow connected to Jase's gut, and she was on him again, scratching at his face and chest.

She didn't stop until someone tackled her to the ground and cuffed her.

twenty-eight

. . .

IT TOOK A WHILE, but eventually, everyone stopped screaming. The cops calmed down and let Jase explain the situation—albeit from the floor in cuffs.

Stella sat between Jase and Travis, wrists cuffed like some kind of vigilante chain gang. Jenny and Cal were in the kitchen, speaking to a female officer in hushed tones.

He'd kept his cool when he saw Stella cuffed and on the floor, but she could've sworn she saw a flicker of amusement in his eyes —like he was proud of her, even now.

The bloodied asshole was already en route to the hospital, a cop riding shotgun just in case. The rest of them were left to answer for what happened. But one look at Jenny's face, and even the most hardened officer softened.

"You gonna behave now?" one of them asked as he removed Stella's cuffs.

"Yes," she mumbled, rolling her aching shoulders, pins and needles buzzing down her arms.

Jase helped her to her feet, and she made a beeline for Jenny, wrapping her in a fierce hug.

"Are you okay?"

Jenny shook her head and wiped at her face, tears streaking the smeared makeup beneath her swollen lip.

"Your friend's lucky you all got here so fast," one of the officers said, voice low and solemn. "That could've ended a lot worse."

Stella's stomach turned. A wave of nausea rushed up her throat, hot and bitter.

Cal saw it. He moved in behind her, slipping a hand under her elbow for support. She offered a grateful smile but kept her eyes on Jenny. She needed the comfort more.

"What now?" Jenny asked, her voice tiny.

"The paramedics said your lip should heal fine," one EMT offered gently. "But it'd be smart to have it looked at—"

"No!" Jenny flinched. "Please don't make me go there. Not if he's there. I can't."

It took a bit of convincing, but the cops and medics finally agreed. Stella promised to keep an eye on the swelling, to clean the cut properly, and to stay close.

"She's in shock," one officer murmured once they were out of earshot. "But the adrenaline's gonna wear off. When it does, it'll hit her hard. She's gonna need someone."

"She's coming home with me," Stella said, brushing her own tears away. "I won't leave her side."

"Hey," Jase said, touching her elbow gently as the officer walked away. "You good?"

Without thinking, Stella pulled him into a hug, then did the same with Travis. She took both their hands and swallowed hard.

"Thank you. You probably saved her life. I don't even know how to—"

"Don't," Travis cut in with a dry chuckle. "It was our fucking pleasure. Now, how about you grab some clothes for your friend, and we'll take you both home?"

She nodded and stepped into Jenny's bedroom. She grabbed a duffel from the floor and began filling it with whatever was clean and soft. But halfway through, her hands started shaking.

"Hey," Cal's voice came from behind. He moved in slowly, wrapping his arms around her waist and pulling her back to him.

She let her head rest against his chest. His kiss found her temple, gentle and grounding.

"She's gonna be okay."

Stella let out a shuddering breath. "Is she?"

"She's staying with you. She's got all of us now. You saw what happened tonight—if that guy so much as breathes in her direction, we'll break his fucking legs."

She tensed. "You know that's not how it works. Guys like him always walk. Even if there's a record, even if this wasn't the first time—"

Cal cupped her face, brushing his thumbs under her eyes.

"Then we make damn sure he doesn't try it again. He shows up, we make it clear. *Very* clear. And I'm pretty sure Trav wants another round anyway. Jase had most of the fun. You too," he added with a ghost of a smile.

"Funny," she muttered, her voice dry with exhaustion as she stepped closer.

She reached for his hand, fingers brushing his, but then heard footsteps. Instinctively, she pulled away.

Cal's face fell as Travis stepped into the room.

"Hey. You ready? Your friend's itching to get the hell out of here."

"Um…"

"We're good," Cal answered tightly. His voice had a clipped edge she hadn't heard before.

Back in the living room, Jenny hadn't moved. She sat beside Jase now, his arm around her as she blinked through the cop's questions.

"She's done," Stella said quietly. "Can this wait until tomorrow?"

The officer nodded. "We just need a few more pictures."

"I'll stick around," Jase said. "Once the cops clear out, I'll get a couple of guys over to fix the door. You two get out of here."

"I'll stay too," Travis added, glancing around at the wreckage. "Might be able to tidy up if they give the okay."

Stella couldn't speak. The tears choked her again, lodged in her throat.

Jenny tried to say something, too, but her voice cracked. Instead, she stood and pulled both brothers into a hug, her thanks pressed into their shoulders.

Then she turned to Cal, who opened his arm and tucked her into his side. Together, they walked out the door.

Stella glanced back at the two men standing in the ruins of Jenny's home. They gave her a nod, quiet and solid.

And she followed her best friend out into the night, knowing this would be the start of a long, hard road—but at least she wasn't on it alone.

twenty-nine

. . .

CAL DROVE them to Stella's Airbnb in charged silence. Jenny sat in the backseat with her head on Stella's shoulder, sobbing quietly the entire way.

Stella kept her arms around her friend, fighting back her own tears. The thought of losing Jenny—her Jenny—was almost too much to bear. Every time she thought about what might've happened if Cal and his brothers hadn't shown up, her stomach twisted.

Twice, she caught Cal's eyes in the rearview mirror. The way he looked at her—equal parts anger, worry, and something heart-breakingly gentle—nearly shattered her.

And even in that moment, she hated herself for thinking about what had happened between them. What she might've ruined.

Keep it together. Just a little longer.

At the apartment, Jenny let Stella help her undress. She peeled off the bloodstained shirt and jeans and tossed them in the trash without a glance. Then Stella ran a hot bath, heavy with salts and bubbles, and helped her friend climb in. As Jenny lowered herself into the water, Stella spotted a purple bruise blooming along her ribs.

Her throat tightened, but she didn't say anything. She just stayed beside her, waiting.

And then the tears came again.

"Stella, I—" Jenny choked out, unable to form words, her whole body shaking.

Stella didn't speak. She just leaned over and wrapped both arms around her, holding her tightly, one hand in her wet hair, the other steady across her back. They stayed like that until the water cooled and the shaking slowed.

Eventually, Stella whispered, "Come on. Let's get you to bed."

Jenny nodded wordlessly, letting herself be wrapped in a thick robe before they stepped out of the bathroom. In the kitchen, Cal was waiting, sleeves rolled, something gently bubbling on the stove. Paper bags were lined up on the counter.

He turned when he saw them and offered a soft smile. "Anybody want tea?"

Jenny cleared her throat. "Actually... yeah. Tea would be nice."

Stella nodded, then guided her friend into the bedroom. The sound of the kettle clicking on and mugs clinking filled the air behind them.

He stayed. That has to mean something.

The bed was unmade, covers twisted from the night before. Jenny didn't care—she crawled under them and lay her head in Stella's lap. A few minutes later, Cal appeared in the doorway with two steaming mugs. He hesitated, then crossed the room and set them on the nightstand.

He crouched beside Stella, brushing a tear from her cheek with his thumb.

Jenny stirred, pushing herself up. "Tea?"

"Green tea and raspberry," Cal said, handing her a cup. "It was all they had."

"Thank you." She held the mug in both hands, breathing in the steam before glancing up. "Thank you. For everything."

Before Stella could even process it, Cal was sitting on the bed.

He gently took the mug from Jenny's hands and pulled her into a hug. She folded into him like she'd been waiting for it all night. Stella couldn't hear what he whispered to her, but she saw Jenny's hand fist in his shirt—and heard the soft, broken sob that followed.

When Jenny finally sat back, she reached out for Stella's hand. "I don't know what would've happened if you hadn't come. Please thank your brothers for me. You will, right?"

"Of course," Cal said. "And like I told you earlier—you call us anytime. Doesn't matter when. One of us will be there."

"Careful," Jenny said, managing a tired chuckle. "You might regret that offer."

"Not a chance," he said with a smile.

"You should sleep," Stella murmured, shifting beside her. "We can talk more tomorrow."

"You don't have to stay," Jenny said. "Just knowing you're in the next room is enough."

"I don't mind—"

"Stells," she interrupted gently. "I'm okay. I needed that bath, I needed the panic. But now… I just need sleep."

Stella kissed her forehead and stood, pausing only to leave the door open a crack. Then she moved through the dark living room and slipped onto the small balcony.

Cal followed silently, only realizing why when he saw the tears streaming down her face.

"I c–can't let her h–hear me," she choked.

Without a word, he wrapped her in his arms.

"She could've died," Stella sobbed.

Cal stiffened. "But she didn't. She's safe now. And he's in jail. He's not coming near her again."

She let out a bitter laugh. "You don't really believe that, do you?"

Cal exhaled slowly and cupped her cheeks. "We have to believe it. And we have to be ready if we're wrong. I already told her to set up a group text shortcut. One button, and all three of us will be there."

"It might not be enough," Stella whispered. "Next time, he might—"

"You can't live in 'next time,'" he said gently. "You'll drown in it."

He kissed the corners of her eyes, wiping the tears with his thumbs.

"The cops have him. She's not alone. She has you. She has us. And maybe…" He hesitated. "Maybe she should move. Somewhere safer. Somewhere new."

Stella stepped back, arms crossing. "Her whole life—her neighborhood, her job, her coffee shop—is ruined because one pathetic man couldn't take a 'no.'"

"I know," Cal said softly. "I hate it too. But she's lucky. And she's got people who'll fight for her. That's more than most."

Stella wiped at her cheeks, her breath finally steadying.

"Thank you. You didn't even hesitate."

He smirked. "What can I say? We've got that unearned white man confidence. And we're bigger than one piece-of-shit with a bruised ego."

She managed a laugh. Then her face shifted—serious again.

"And about… before. When—"

"Forget it," Cal said quickly, pulling her in. "I already did."

thirty

. . .

AFTER THE INCIDENT, Jenny moved full-time into Stella's Airbnb. No longer feeling safe in her own home, she was grateful for the sanctuary, and Stella was eager to offer it. They'd always supported each other. Jenny had been Stella's rock after losing her sister, and now Stella was determined to return the kindness.

With Jenny there, Stella rearranged her life to support her friend. She synced their schedules, ensuring she was home before Jenny and only left after she'd gone for the day. She checked in frequently, and they met for lunch nearly every day—now outside Jenny's office rather than at their usual spots—to maintain a comforting routine.

That left little time for Cal.

He'd seemed to mean it when he said to forget what happened at Jenny's place. And that night, he'd held her on the couch while Jenny slept in the bedroom, not leaving until Jenny woke and told him she was okay.

He called and texted, offering a steady presence without pressing for more attention. He knew Jenny needed time and didn't once make Stella feel guilty about staying home with her friend. He even offered to go with them to the police station, if and when the time came.

But Stella couldn't shake the feeling that this was a turning point for them.

Cal had wanted to tell his brothers they were a couple, but she'd said no, preferring to keep things private. And now, they weren't even seeing each other at the house. Instead, she'd been calling and emailing, which his brothers were c'd on.

So, no chance of any funny business.

But then, after almost two weeks, when things had calmed down, Cal sent Stella a text that lifted her spirits—and her libido.

> Hey, how's Jenny?
>
> A little bird told me you might be free to come by later? The crew should be gone by around 7.
>
> No pressure. I get it if you can't make it.

It was a booty call, she knew, and one she was more than happy to RSVP 'yes' to. Jenny was having dinner with her folks and planned to stay at their place overnight. Now Stella knew why, and it only made her love her more.

Rushing home from work, she showered and blew out her hair, adding a little blush to her cheeks and even putting on eyeliner. She chose a black dress that was summery but tight. It hugged her waist and made her tits look incredible.

Then, wanting to set him on fire, she chose a matching set of crotchless red panties and a lace bra.

The excitement built up on her drive over. And in truth, she was just as eager to see the house. The boys had been sending photos, but it wasn't the same as seeing it with her own eyes, which lit up when she pulled onto her new street.

It looked incredible—the finished driveway, the new facade, a peek at the landscaping.

Too bad the construction crew was still out front, killing the mood she'd been building since her shower.

Well, damn.

She waited in the car, thighs pressed together, not about to strut through a half-constructed house with her dress barely covering anything.

It took around twenty minutes for the place to finally go quiet.

Stella peeked up and down the street, then hustled inside, tugging her dress down as she called out, "Hello? Cal?"

No answer.

She checked her phone, assuming he was running late. But there was no text or missed call.

Huh. Wierd.

The disappointment didn't last. Instead, she smiled and took the chance to look around. The kitchen was almost finished, the walls were all in place, and the deck was about halfway done. Ascending the stairs, she ran her hand up the freshly painted wall and sighed at the sight of her master bedroom.

But before she could look closer, she heard a truck pull into the driveway. She darted into the bathroom, heart racing.

"Hello? Anybody here?" a muffled voice called from downstairs.

"Up here," she called, choosing to lose the dress completely so they could get straight to the good part.

At first, she panicked a little, wondering how best to greet him. But then, knowing how much he liked to fuck her from behind, she chose to lean forward into the window, her ass out like an invitation.

Cal's footsteps got closer, and when he opened the door, she heard him heave out a breath. Stella laughed, loving the effect she had on him.

Swirling her hips, she whispered, "What are you waiting for?"

He was on her in seconds, fingers cold but firm. He stroked between her legs, slipping inside with ease. She gasped, reaching back to guide his other hand to her breast.

He pulled the bra aside. One hand gripped her nipple, the other teased her clit. But he wasn't gentle. She could tell he was excited as his pace quickened and his grip on her nipple hardened.

To keep things moving, she tucked her hand behind her back and found the button at the front of his pants. It came away quickly, and she managed to get inside, finding his rock-hard cock fighting to be freed.

Cal let out a gasp of his own when she squeezed, trying to stroke at the odd angle. With his fingers firmly on her clit, she didn't want to turn, but she needed more. She needed him inside.

They didn't hear the front door open and close.

They didn't hear the boots on the stairs.

And they didn't hear him call out her name.

"Oh, Cal," she breathed, turning and pulling his face to hers.

The second their lips met, she knew. Her eyes popped open, and she reared back.

"Cal?" Jase asked, totally confused.

"Jase?" Stella gasped.

"What the *fuck*?" Cal snarled.

Stella stumbled back and scrambled to find her dress. Jase stood inches away, his dick halfway out and her juices on his fingers. Cal was in the doorway, rage on his face, his fists already balled

"Cal, wait—"

But it was too late. He charged forward and caught his brother on the side. They stumbled into the vanity, fists flying.

"Wait. Please!" Stella tried, but she knew it was no use.

Cal got in a few hits, and then Jase did too. He knocked his brother off balance with an uppercut, taking the momentary break to try and calm things down.

"Bro, I don't know what the fuck is—"

Cal charged again, shoving his shoulder into Jase's stomach, lifting him up, and rushing them both back until they hit the wall. The mirror smashed, and both men fell to their knees.

Stella ignored the fists and got between them, her foot snagging a piece of glass. She fumbled into Jase, put her hand on his shoulder, and swore. It wasn't until her eyes met his that she remembered she was still in her underwear.

"Stop! *Both of you!* This was a mistake! Cal—*look at me!*"

Cal turned. His chest heaved. His eyes fell to her hand—still braced on Jase's arm.

That was it.

His shoulders dropped. Something cold passed over his face.

Then he turned and walked out without a word.

thirty-one

. . .

"CAL WAI— OW!" Stella tried to follow, but the glass in her foot stopped her in her tracks.

"Whoa, Stella. Stop." Jase sighed and struggled to his feet. "Don't move—you'll make it worse."

He extended his arm to steady her, his eyes quickly scanning from her bleeding bare feet to the sink. Gently, he scooped her up in his arms and carried her across the room. With careful movements, he set her on the counter and lifted her injured foot to assess the damage.

Then his eyes dropped—and widened—when he realized just how little she was wearing.

"Shit. Sorry. I...uh..." He scanned the room for something to offer her, then gave up and pulled off his own shirt.

"Jase, what—"

"It's for...your..." he stammered, holding the shirt between her legs.

Suddenly painfully aware of how exposed she was, Stella snatched the shirt and covered up.

"Right. Thanks."

Flushed, confused, and still clearly aroused, Jase reached for her foot. "May I?"

Stella nodded, crying out in pain when he touched the wound.

Fuck. Fuck. Fuck.

"Just...hold on."

Jase put her foot down and left the room. She thought about jumping down to find her dress—until she remembered how short it was. No way it would cover anything in her current position.

A few minutes later, he returned with a light, a first aid kit, and a flannel shirt. Stella smiled her thanks and shrugged it on, clenching the T-shirt between her thighs.

Jase set the light to illuminate only her foot and carefully pulled the glass free. Then, he meticulously cleaned the wound and wrapped it tight. When he was done, he turned the light off and stepped back, hands in his pockets.

With some of the pain relieved, Stella felt a whole new wave of regret and guilt.

"Uh, Jase? You okay?"

She could see a busted lip and what looked like a soon-to-be black eye. But mostly, he just looked pissed.

"I don't know, Stella. I'm a little fucking confused."

She winced. "I'm so sorry," she began, sitting upright as he stepped away. "I thought you were..."

"You thought I was Cal. Yeah, I kinda pieced that together."

Finally, he brought his dark eyes up to hers and softened. He shook his head and shrugged. "I shoulda known."

"No...I. Fuck. This is on me."

Stella reached for his hand, pulling him closer. She took a look at his eye and rummaged in the first aid kit. He flinched as she cleaned the blood away, but smiled when she was done.

"Thanks."

"Don't thank me. I can't believe I let this happen. I'm so sorry, Jase. I'm so so—"

"This isn't your fault." Jase cracked his neck. "I guess it's not really anybody's fault. It's just a shitty fucking mistake and...and..." He ran a hand over his face, rubbing his brows in frustration. "I don't know what to do now. Cal's gonna...I don't even know. I've never seen him like that. Like, *ever*."

Stella chewed her cheek and pushed off the counter, tugging the shirt as low as it would go. She put her foot down carefully, feeling red hot pain when she tried to put weight on it.

Gripping the vanity for support, she said, "We should've told you. Cal wanted to. I just... I didn't want you all thinking I was some kind of slut."

"Your sex life isn't our business." Jase hunched his shoulders in defeat and looked around. "We work for you, right? I was an idiot to think—"

"Don't say that."

Stella's neck flushed as she wondered what he must've thought walking in that night. Her car parked out front. Her body practically on display. It was an open invitation.

She licked her lips, remembering how he'd felt. The callouses on his fingers racking over her clit. His firm grip on her breasts as he sank his fingers inside.

And his dick.

Jesus. He was huge. Thicker than Cal, maybe even longer.

It had been rock solid under her grip. And while Stella was very likely in love with Cal, she couldn't help but wonder how it would've felt—how *he* would've felt.

Jase was big with huge arms and a round, tight ass. So yes, she'd found herself looking at him while he worked. And yes, she'd even let her mind wander in the last couple of weeks during her solo sessions.

And now?

A small part of her wanted him to touch her again. To feel his fingers inside and his cock in her mouth.

But Cal...

Cal had awakened a sexual side of Stella she never knew existed. Nobody had made her cum the way he could, and nobody had ever made her feel as sexy.

Looking at Jase now, it all became clear.

Yes, he was undeniably gorgeous and, no doubt, incredible in bed. But there was one obvious reason she was so attracted to him.

He looks just like Cal.

And it was Cal she wanted. She'd been so horny for the last couple of weeks without him that her pussy had taken over. She'd been so lost in finally being touched that she hadn't noticed how different Jase had felt. Which was probably the shittiest part of all.

"Jase, I...I don't know what to say. I don't think I can apologize enough for—"

"For *me* wanting you?"

Stella froze.

"I've thought about it. I've thought about you and this" —he waved his hand between them and took a step closer— "since we started this job."

Tugging the hem of the shirt with one hand and pulling the top together with the other, Stella stepped back until her thighs touched the vanity.

Jase's mouth hardened into a flat, resigned line as he watched her retreat.

"Honestly?" he continued, the intensity in his eyes softening. "I kinda thought you maybe had a thing for me, too. You were always around. Always kind. I guess I read into it. I thought maybe I caught you flirting a couple of times, and then when I came in just now, I— shit. I just figured you were waiting for me."

In spite of everything, Stella blushed and smiled.

She'd thought he was Cal, which was why she was so into it. But Jase had been just as enthusiastic, and he knew it was her. How long had he been interested?

"Um..."

"Look, I don't know what you and Cal have," he interrupted. "If it's just a sex thing or if…" He trailed off, looking into her eyes for an answer. "But I would kick myself if I didn't at least shoot my shot."

Stella gulped.

What the fuck is happening?

"Jase," she whispered. "I'm really sorry. But I think…Cal and I have been…uh…"

He offered a sheepish smile and a shrug, his hands lifted in a gesture that said, 'I got it.' Giving her space, he ran his fingers through his hair and exhaled deeply.

"So, what now?"

Stella hugged herself tightly, feeling exposed. "I don't know. I think…I think I love your brother. And I'm mortified about all this."

She pushed off from the vanity, caught in a tug-of-war inside her head. Part of her wanted to reach out and touch him, just to bridge the gap, but she knew that wouldn't be right.

"I'm sorry if I made you feel like I was…if I led you on. Maybe I was being too friendly. Maybe even flirty, I—"

"No, don't do that," Jase said, wagging his finger. "You were nice and friendly, and I just, I don't know, got caught up. And now, I guess I know why. You were being nice because you wanted us to like you. Right?"

Her cheeks blushed, and she nodded. "Yes. I figured if you already liked me as a boss, you'd like me as your brother's girlfriend. But I guess I overdid it, huh?"

The room fell silent. Jase pulled out his phone and paced to the window to glance outside.

"I should go," he said eventually. "Need a hand getting to your car? Or want me to drive you?"

Stella shook her head. "I'm gonna call Cal."

Jase nodded.

"Are we okay?" she asked, her voice tinged with worry as he turned to leave.

"If I'm being honest… it's gonna be hard not to think about how incredible you felt."

Stella clenched, her nipples still aching from his touch.

"But I'll try. And I promise I won't make it weird."

They exchanged an awkward hug, and then he was gone. As he drove off, Stella couldn't help but feel uneasy. He said he'd speak to Cal and told her not to worry.

But how can I not worry?

Alone in the dark, she ripped off the shirt and found her dress. Then she grabbed her phone and dialed Cal, crossing her fingers that he'd answer.

He didn't, of course.

With a shaky breath, she typed out a text instead.

> Cal, please. I'm still at the house. Jase is gone
>
> I just need you to let me explain
>
> I thought he was you. I had no idea
>
> Please, Cal. Come back so we can talk
>
> I'll wait all night if I have to.

With her phone clutched in her hand, Stella left the bathroom and made her way downstairs. She tiptoed outside and settled into one of the chairs left by the crew, her eyes glued to the phone's screen, silently pleading for a reply.

thirty-two

. . .

A SUDDEN HAND on her shoulder jolted Stella awake, nearly sending her tumbling from the chair. She whipped around, her vision blurry, as she tried desperately to blink away the remnants of a nightmare.

Please tell me it was just a bad dream.

But she knew it wasn't.

"Cal?" she murmured, blinking up at the shadowed figure above her.

"Should I be wearing a name tag?" he snapped. "Might help for your next booty call."

It sounded like a joke, but his voice was like ice. He turned and went back inside, not offering her a hand.

As Stella slowly regained her bearings, she tried to gauge the time. It was still dark, which meant she hadn't been out there long. Her hands fumbled over the dirt until they found her phone. She tapped the screen. There were no texts, but she saw it was 2:12 a.m.

She'd been there for close to four hours.

She pushed to her feet, but pain shot through her as she put weight on her injured foot. Gritting her teeth, she hobbled toward the house. Before she could reach the sliding door, it opened, and Cal appeared with a blanket in his hand.

"Thanks," she said, wishing he would look her in the eyes.

But when he saw her limp, his expression shifted. He stepped in quickly and tucked an arm under hers, taking her weight.

"What the fuck happened?" he asked angrily.

"Oh, it was... the mirror. From the bathroom. I stepped on some glass."

Cal stopped and finally met her eyes, his brow furrowed in worry. "Shit. Fuck, I'm...I'm sorry."

He helped her to the temporary kitchen table, where invoices and plans were scattered under a lamp. He took the seat across from her and clicked on the light. It revealed his black eye and bruised knuckles.

"Cal, please let me explain. I need you to know—"

"I know," he interrupted, raising a hand to stop her. "I talked to Jase."

You did what?

Stella's stomach flipped. "Okay. I mean, that's good. Wait—you *just* talked, though, right?"

He gave a dry laugh and glanced down at his bruised hand. "Yeah. Just talked."

"I'm so sorry, Cal. I just...I don't know what to say."

With a sigh, he ran his hand over his face, rubbing his eyebrows the same way Jase had a few hours earlier.

"I know it's not your fault. Jase explained how you... He told me you didn't know it was him. And I guess we're similar, right? In the dark, sure. I get it."

"I knew the second I kissed him," Stella said quickly. "I knew, and I stopped it."

"Stells, I..." Cal looked away, unable to meet her eyes. "The logical part of my brain can see this for what it was. I can see it as a mistake, and I know you didn't...*want* him."

"No, Cal. I don't have *any* feelings for Jase. At all!"

"He told me he saw you—half naked, all worked up—and he

just... reacted. And honestly?" Cal laughed bitterly. "I get it. You're impossible to resist. But..."

"But?" Stella pressed when he was quiet for too long.

"I just need a little time," he confessed, his voice faltering. "Because the other part of my brain can't help but think about his hands on you. He wants you, Stella. He didn't say it, but he wouldn't have... Not if he didn't already think about you that way. And I *know* you didn't know, but I can't make that right yet. Because you let him kiss you. You let him put his hands on you. I don't even know how far it went—or could've gone. And that's what kills me."

Cal spread his hands in a helpless gesture, then sighed again and clasped them behind his head.

"I can't be with you right now. I can't do this and put what happened aside."

A tear slid down her cheek. She nodded, even though her chest was splitting open.

"I get it. I do, I get all of it. Maybe I should've known. I should've *felt* that it wasn't you. And I can't make it go away, but I need you to hear me when I say that I don't have *any* feelings for Jase."

She hesitated, wondering whether or not to tell him the truth.

I guess it won't hurt now.

"As for Jase, I...I wish I could say I had no idea he thought about me like that, but..."

Cal's jaw twitched. "But?"

"I guess I caught him looking at me a couple of times, smiling and being...overly friendly. Maybe? I don't— I *never* led him on, Cal. I swear, I was friendly but professional, and I always made sure to...I don't know, just not be suggestive around him—or anyone. At least, I think...I don't..."

Cal pursed his lips. "Be honest. Is that why you didn't want to tell them about us? Because of this thing with Jase?"

"What? No!" Stella cried, her hands coming down on the table.

"No, Cal. I swear. I just thought he was flirty like some guys are. I didn't think it was a crush or whatever."

Reaching out, Stella put her hand under his, carefully avoiding the bruising. But she could see they weren't going to resolve this. Cal could barely look her in the eye.

"Look, I don't expect you to forgive me tonight, and I get that you need space." She pulled her hand back and cleared her throat. "So I'll give you space. If anything comes up with the house, have Travis call me."

Cal nodded. "Okay."

Okay? Shit. Not *okay*.

Struggling to her feet, Stella limped to the door. She sniffed back tears and cleared her throat, turning one last time before she left.

"I've never felt like this about anyone. I've never felt so alive in my whole life, and that's all down to you," she said, pausing in the doorway. "I think I...I think I might be in love with you. So, I'm willing to wait, Cal. I'm happy to give you time and space, and if you decide you don't want me anymore, I'll accept that. But if you can forgive me and find a way to get past this..."

She stopped, hoping he would turn her way. He didn't, his eyes on his hands as she spoke.

"If you want to be with me, I'll be here. I'll be waiting because I'm not willing to just walk away from you. I don't think I could even if I tried."

She waited. One second. Two. Still nothing.

Her throat closed up. She turned and walked out the door, as fast as her injured foot would allow, holding herself together just long enough to reach her car. The second the door closed, she sobbed into the steering wheel until her throat was raw. Then she started the car and left.

thirty-three

. . .

CAL KEPT his eyes fixed on the table as Stella stood and limped to the door. His heart damn near burst out of his chest when she said she might be in love with him, yet he couldn't bring himself to look at her—not until the sound of her car door slamming shook him out of the haze.

It snapped him back to reality, and he hurried to the front of the house, knocking the chair over as he moved.

But something held him back.

Fingers poised on the cool brass of the doorknob, Cal paused and glanced out the window. There, under the dim glow of the console light, he saw Stella hunched over the steering wheel. He watched, heart aching, as she sobbed and shook, her cries echoing in the quiet until they gradually faded into the surrounding darkness.

Part of him—a big fucking part—wanted to run out there, to pull her into his arms and promise that everything would be okay. He wanted to carry her inside, lay her down on the couch, and kiss her until all the pain disappeared. He wanted her to fall asleep with his hands on her skin and his name in her mouth.

Instead, he just watched.

Watched her cry. Watched her breathe. Watched her finally start the car and go.

And all he could think was: *She's going to bed with my brother's hands still on her. With Jase's mouth still on her skin.*

After the fight, Cal drove home. He knew Jase would come. He didn't even take off his jacket—just sat on the edge of the couch, beer in hand, waiting.

The knock came sooner than expected, which he tried to take as a good sign.

He didn't stay with her.

The moment he swung the door open, Cal felt his fists clench involuntarily, his muscles tightening in anticipation of what might come next. He flashed to the image of Jase's hands between Stella's thighs, and the only thing he wanted was to beat him bloody.

But he kept it together. Barely.

"Beer's cold," he muttered, turning away.

Jase grabbed a bottle from the fridge and leaned against the island. They both drank in silence, eyes fixed on the floor.

The quiet stretched uncomfortably before Jase finally sighed. Cal couldn't help but roll his eyes in frustration.

This is so fucked.

After a few tense moments, Cal's patience wore thin.

"You gonna tell me you didn't know it was her?"

"Didn't know?" Jase scoffed. "Of course I knew. What I *didn't* know was that you were already fucking her."

Cal's jaw clenched. "Would that've stopped you?"

"Fuck you." Jase slammed his bottle on the counter, his finger jabbing angrily in the air. "Don't act like I'm some woman-stealing asshole. I walked in, saw her half-naked, and reacted. I had no idea you two were—whatever the hell you are. I thought she was waiting for me. I thought she—"

"What?" Cal stood and squared up to his slightly taller brother. "You thought she *what*?"

Jase hesitated, taking a step back and another swig of his beer.

"Shit, man. I thought she knew it was me. My truck was

outside, and I just…why would I think anything else? But she didn't, bro. She freaked when she saw me."

Cal knew his brother. Knew Jase wasn't the kind of guy to chase after someone his brother was with. He just wasn't the type.

But that just made the whole thing harder.

"Shit, Jase. Fuck!"

"How long?" Jase asked.

Cal turned his back and wandered to the patio doors. "Since before we started. Since she fired Marco."

Jase let out a low whistle. "Damn. Okay. But why lie about it? Why not just tell us?"

Unsure of the answer, Cal turned back to his brother. "She didn't want you guys thinking…I don't know. Thinking she was slutty or something. And then I guess we both kind of liked sneaking around."

In the kitchen light, he could see a bruise coming in on Jase's eye, the split in his lip. This wasn't their first fight, but it was the first fueled by real rage. Not just you-took-my-truck-without-asking angry, but I'm-gonna-fucking-kill-you rage.

Trav's gonna be so pissed.

"What now?" Jase asked, reaching into the fridge. He pulled out two beers and popped them open while Cal considered their next steps.

"I guess we just…go to work tomorrow and try to act normal."

He took the beer and held it out. The bottles clinked, the sound ringing out like the closing bell of a boxing match.

"That even possible?"

Cal shut his eyes and rubbed the bridge of his nose.

Is it?

"Look, right now, I'm pissed. I'm fucking fuming, and I wanna smash this bottle over your goddamn head. But I won't do that. I won't do that because I know you didn't do this to hurt me. I *know* you didn't know about Stella and me, and I know you would never touch her if you did."

Jase tried to ease the tension. "I mean, she *is* fucking hot, bro…"

Cal's hand clenched around the glass.

"Too soon?"

This motherfucker.

Despite everything, Cal barked out a laugh. He could never stay mad at Jase. Not really.

"Just give me a minute, okay? Let me get right with this and we'll be good."

Jase put a hand on Cal's shoulder and nodded. "I can do that." He finished his beer and stood to leave, but paused at the doorway.

"She's at the house, waiting for you," he said softly.

Cal lifted his bottle in a silent goodbye.

He sat alone in the dark with the empty bottle in his hand for over an hour, trying to talk himself down. Then, he grabbed his keys and got in the truck—but instead of heading straight to the house, he drove aimlessly around the city. Taking every turn *away* from her.

He thought if he waited long enough, he could get it all out of his system. Say the right things. Be the man she deserved.

But when he pulled up and saw her there, curled in a chair, alone, mascara streaked and lips trembling, he knew he wasn't ready.

Not yet.

Because no matter how much he told himself it wasn't her fault… he couldn't forget that she hadn't known. She couldn't feel the difference between them.

She let Jase touch her.

She let Jase kiss her.

And she didn't know.

And for some reason, that destroyed him more than anything else.

"I can't be with you right now," he'd said, his heart aching with every word. "I can't do this and put what happened aside."

Cal could see she was heartbroken, but he managed to keep it together. When she got up to leave, he shifted, wanting to help her on her injured foot. But then she turned and drove a dagger through his heart.

She was in love with him. Or, at least, falling. And she was willing to wait.

"If you want to be with me, I'll be here. I'll be waiting because I'm not willing to just walk away from you. I don't think I could even if I tried."

She left, and he told himself he just needed a few days. He was sure could move on once his temper calmed. But a few days turned into a week. And that week turned into two. And then three.

Three weeks of avoiding her and short, quick conversations with Jase. Three weeks of not seeing her and blaming his brother every day for it.

This is all his fucking fault.

Instead of talking to his brother like a grown-up, Cal kept his head down and worked as hard as he could to finish the house. Just being there was a trigger, and he hadn't set foot in the bathroom since that night.

Travis sensed the tension but kept his obvious frustrations to himself, and Jase did his best to give his brother room to breathe.

Stella did, too. She didn't try to get in touch and made her visits to the house infrequent. Instead of just showing up, she sent a text in the group chat, knowing he'd see it and choose to either leave or stay and face her.

Each time her name popped up on his phone, he thought about staying. He thought about calling her, about reaching out to bridge the gap between them.

He wanted to. Shit, it was all he wanted. *She* was all he wanted. But a mix of pride, unresolved anger, and maybe even fear kept him from the one thing he wanted the most.

So he didn't go see her. Or email or text. Or show up at the house until he was sure she'd left. And almost every night, Cal went to bed wishing he had the balls to just fucking call her.

thirty-four

. . .

HER SKIN GLISTENED in the sunlight as she stepped out of the water, shaking her hair and tits as she moved toward him. The little white bikini covered just enough to be legal, but left nothing to the imagination. He saw the tan line curved around her crotch and the edge of a nipple peeking out from the left cup.

Cal's dick stiffened as she sauntered over and leaned across his lounger, her cleavage inches from his face.

"I just need the sunblock." She smirked. "You mind?"

Stella handed him the bottle and perched on the edge of the lounger, slowly pulling her wet hair off her shoulders.

Licking his lips, Cal shuffled back and sat upright so he could reach every inch of her. He squirted the cream into his palm and rubbed his hands together before touching her skin. She let out a deep, contented sigh as his fingers skillfully massaged her neck, kneading the tension from her shoulders.

Tugging at the strings of her bikini top, Cal slid them aside, baring her entire back to him. He worked his way down, loving how warm and smooth she felt in the sun. She hummed under his touch and wiggled when his hands trailed around her waist.

Leaning back into him, Stella guided his hands lower, letting his fingers graze her bikini bottoms. Her top clung to her breasts, but it peeled away easily, revealing pert, hard nipples. Cal groaned, rolling them between his slick fingers.

He could feel his cock straining against his shorts, but he wasn't done touching her.

Slowly, he lowered his right hand, found the edge of her bikini bottoms, and carefully tucked his fingers under the wet fabric. With just his index finger, he slid into her, gently testing her until she gasped.

Still toying with her breasts, Cal added a second finger below. He stroked gently at first, then with more intent, until she was wet and panting under his touch.

When he finally drove his fingers inside her, Stella twitched. He found her clit and pressed firmly, making her whimper as she clung to the lounger.

Stella moaned and gripped the edge of the bed while he stroked over her slick pussy. He didn't stop when she said his name. Instead, he picked up the pace, pushing her until she could hardly breathe.

Before she could cum, he withdrew and grabbed her hair, turning her face to his for a kiss. She stood quickly, yanked her bikini bottoms down, and straddled him.

The smirk on her face drove him crazy as she shuffled back, pulling at his swim shorts until his cock sprang free. He reached for her, wanting to draw her face to his. But she held back, lowered her head, and licked the tip of his erect length.

"Stella," he warned, breathless.

She looked up through her lashes and sucked him deeper. Her hand wrapped around the base as she bobbed her head, taking him to the root again and again.

When she came up for air, Cal grabbed her chin and pulled her in. Stella crawled up his body, kissed him hard, and then reached between them to guide him inside.

Cal lifted his head to suck a nipple between his lips, fingers finding her clit again. He pressed hard, pushing her over the edge. She came with a cry, her hips jerking as she clenched around him.

Cal followed, shuddering into her as she rose and fell, her hips twitching under his grasp.

"Fuck, Stells," he mumbled into her chest

She leaned back, hands on his chest, eyes locked with his.

Fuck, I love this girl.

————

When he woke up, Cal was hard as a rock. It'd been almost a month since he'd last been with Stella, and the dreams were getting worse. Every night, she was in his head—naked, moaning, riding him—and every morning, he woke up with a throbbing erection and no relief.

Exhausted and frustrated, he threw the covers off and stomped to the bathroom. Under scalding water, he angrily jerked off, trying to focus on her face, her voice, her moans.

That first time, with her telling him about her dreams and him finger fucking her until her knees went weak. Or the time in the van, her ass in the air and the taste of her pussy when she was wet.

But then the images shifted—her and Jase. Jase's hands on her. Jase inside her.

He tried to shake it off and finally came with a growl, smacking his hand on the tile.

Spent and still aching, he dried off and yanked on a pair of work jeans. Minutes later, he was in the car.

On the way to the house, he grabbed a coffee and a bagel, finishing both as he drove. The radio blared at full volume, the loud music an attempt to drown out his churning, toxic thoughts.

But as he turned the corner near Stella's house, he slammed on the brakes.

Her car was in the driveway.

Fuck. Shit. Fuck!

He pulled out his phone and saw the missed message. She'd texted. He'd ignored it.

His heart raced as he tapped a nervous rhythm on the steering wheel, panic setting in. Travis was there already, he knew, and he was pretty sure he could see Jase's truck further up the road.

The logical side of his brain told him to man up and go inside. But with the sweat on his brow and how he white-knuckled the steering wheel, he knew logic wouldn't win this time.

Seeing Stella was one thing.

Seeing her next to Jase?

Nope.

Cal backed out of the street before anyone could spot him and drove straight to the nearest coffee shop. He ordered a big box of coffee and bought every donut in sight.

By the time he got back, she was gone.

Again.

thirty-five

· · ·

THE CREW WAS happy to see the boss arrive with coffee and donuts. They nodded their thanks—one donut already in their mouths, another stashed for later. If they'd noticed Cal's recent disappearing act, they didn't let on.

Travis, on the other hand, was another story.

He was in the backyard when Cal finally arrived, having heard the happy uproar over free donuts. As Cal stepped outside, Travis was there to greet him, leaning against the gazebo frame with one eyebrow raised and his lips pressed into a tight, unimpressed line.

"You missed the meeting with Stella," he said, waving a clip-board in the air. "She wanted to go over the outdoor space. Changed her mind on the tile."

Cal cleared his throat and handed his brother a coffee. "That was today? Forgot."

"Forgot? I texted you last—"

The backdoor opened again. "Trav, I gotta go grab some…" Jase's voice trailed off when he saw Cal. "Oh. Hey."

Cal gave him a curt nod and half smile before turning toward the side of the house.

Travis's patience finally snapped.

"Stop," he barked. "Fucking stop, Cal."

"Trav, I—"

"You what? Huh?" Travis stepped into the space between his brothers and held up his arms like a referee ready to break up a brawl.

Here we go.

"What the fuck is going on? I've been trying to ignore whatever shit you two have going on, but it's affecting the business. *Our* business. The business we started and the business that's gonna go to fucking hell if you two can't be in the same room."

Jase and Cal stayed quiet, briefly making eye contact before looking back to their shoes like little kids in trouble with dad.

"Okay. Fine." Travis slammed the clipboard onto the floor and clapped his hands together. "My guess? One or both of you fucked Stella, and now you're in some kind of weird soap-opera love triangle. And since Jase's been here, I'm guessing the two of them made the final cut, and you're pissed about it."

Cal gritted his teeth, his fingernails digging into his palms.

They've been together?

"Trav…" Jase started.

"What the fuck does that mean? You've been here? Are you and Stella—?"

"Cal, no. Dude, come on." Jase quickly closed the back door and lowered his voice. "We went over this. It was a mistake—an *innocent* mistake that we both regret. But we didn't…"

"You didn't fuck, I know. But you still…you…shit, Jase." Cal ran a hand over his face and took a few steps forward.

At that, his brothers shifted, ready for a fight.

"Are the two of you talking? Are you…what?"

Jase hesitated. "We're polite. We're friendly. I broke the ice with a bad joke, and we're okay. She's the client, man. Trav can't be the only one she talks to."

"Do you still want her?" Cal pressed, fists clenching. "You wouldn't've touched her like that if you didn't."

Jase glanced nervously at Travis and then back at Cal, clearly unsure how much to say.

"No," he admitted finally. "I don't. But could you blame me if I did?"

Travis looked totally confused but kept quiet. He let them talk but kept his feet steady between them.

Cal sighed. "I guess I can't."

"Yes, I think she's sexy. And did I flirt a little before that night? Sure. And maybe I thought she was flirting back. Wearing those low-cut tops and smiling all the time."

He glanced at Travis, hoping for some backup, but Travis wisely chose to remain neutral.

Resigned, Jase dropped his head. "I thought she knew it was me. But now I know it was all for you. Lucky son of a bitch," he added with a smirk.

Cal's mind drifted unwillingly to that night. Jase's hands on Stella. Her moans. The way she responded without knowing.

It drove him crazy to think she hadn't known it wasn't him.

She should've known…

But the more he looked at his brother, the more he understood. They were too similar in so many ways. The way they walked, dressed, and talked. Everyone had always said they were more like twins.

Shit, they even wore the same deodorant.

He probably smelled like me, too.

"Cal—"

"You're right," Cal whispered, raising his hands in defeat. "You're both right. I've been a dickhead. A childish dickhead."

He turned to Travis and sighed. His brother had probably pieced enough together to understand what had happened, but he still owed him the truth.

"I was fu— *with* Stella since before you guys got involved. We hooked up after she fired Marco and were seeing each other in secret. I wanted to tell you, but she was worried about what you'd think of her," he explained, seeing the wrinkle between Travis's eyebrows. "And there was a...misunderstanding one night. She was waiting for me, but Jase got here first and..."

He stopped, not wanting to go into any more detail.

"Anyway, I haven't been able to stop thinking about it. But," he took a deep breath and grabbed Jase's shoulder. "I can move past it. I can. We're all grown-ups, right?"

Jase slapped a hand on Cal's back and tugged him into a hug.

"I'm sorry, bro."

"I know, man. I know."

Travis stepped in and put a hand on each of their shoulders. "You serious? Because I can't manage this project alone."

Cal nodded and smiled. "We're good."

At least, as good as we can be.

"So...can we get back to business now?" Travis asked, eyebrows raised. "Because I think we might have a new client. And it's a big one."

thirty-six

· · ·

"JUST LET ME DO THE TALKING." Travis pressed the button in the elevator and fixed his tie in the mirror. "You two are the muscle. But they wanna hear the nitty-gritty. The numbers and shit."

Jase laughed. "You calling us dumb?"

"Sounds like it to me, bro," Cal added with a smirk.

"You two got any idea how many man hours this project's gonna take? Got more than one supplier in your phone? No? There's a reason I'm the project manager, and you two knuckle-heads carry the tools."

"Relax, Trav. We got it." Jase mimed locking his lips and throwing away the key. "If they ask how to drill a hole, we'll jump in. Other than that, it's all you."

The three brothers were dressed to impress: freshly dry-cleaned, perfectly tailored suits, ties knotted just right, and designer stubble framing their chiseled jaws.

We look downright presentable. They'd be morons to say no.

The client was waiting in a large conference room. A dozen or so people milled around, stacking papers, straightening chairs, and arranging pastries on a plate. The room smelled like fresh coffee and powdered sugar, and the client—a woman Travis told them had more money than the state of Texas—sat at the end with a phone to her ear, exuding authority and wealth.

A young woman, whom Cal presumed was an assistant, greeted them warmly and showed them to their seats. Soon after, they were each served a cup of coffee and given an empty plate. She pushed the pastries closer for their convenience.

After a few minutes, Ms. Kim hung up the phone and apologized.

"Family matter," she said simply, handing the phone to the person closest.

Travis cleared his throat. "Thank you for taking the time to see us, Ms. Kim. We know we're not a big company, but we're hard workers, and our team is the best. We know everyone in this town, so we can get you what you need at prices you'll love."

Ms. Kim smiled reassuringly, her hands neatly folded on the table. "Call me Caroline. And you've come highly recommended, so there's no need for a sales pitch. Instead, I want to see what you've brought me. I want to know if our...styles match."

Cal's gaze swept the room, half expecting Stella to jump out from behind the ficus. He was more nervous about seeing her than the pitch.

"Well," Travis began, opening his laptop and plugging it into a cable in the center of the table.

The screen at the end of the room flickered to life, displaying the opening slide of his meticulously prepared presentation. He inhaled deeply, poised to deliver the pitch Cal knew he'd rehearsed relentlessly throughout the week.

Caroline chuckled. "Relax, Mr. Morrow. I won't bite."

Travis flexed his hands at his sides. "Right. So we started by visiting the site."

He grabbed the remote and clicked a button, moving the slide onto a few pictures they'd taken.

"She's got good bones. Amazing, really, given how old the building is. These stone walls are solid, and we think they'd make great features. Unfortunately, some areas" —he clicked to the next slide— "are too far gone. But we feel we can recreate the look. If that's what you want, of course."

"Say it is," Caroline prompted. "What would you do with it?"

Travis grinned, finally comfortable. Over the next hour, he laid out their plan for the empty buildings. Ms. Kim had bought a whole block of old factories in the hopes of turning them into a new live-work area for young professionals. Her email said she wanted "to keep the spirit of the buildings but gut what needed to go." She seemed open to ideas, which left the brothers with a lot of room to explore. And they were proud of their pitch.

"So, ultimately, you're looking at 10-15 spaces each on the ground floor. They can be a mix of restaurants, coffee shops, and small stores. Then, the offices above. Probably ten zones would be comfortable. Finally, the lofts and apartments. You can fit between eighty and a hundred in total, depending on whether you want one or two bedrooms. We feel a mix of both would work best, though this area is more for young professionals and couples without kids. That means more one beds than two. And we really think this lot," he highlighted the end building with a laser pointer, "should be a shared working space. They're huge right now for freelancers and bring in a ton of revenue when done right. We have a separate pitch for that if you're interested."

Travis let out a breath, set the remote down, and clasped his hands together, waiting patiently for Caroline to speak. He looked at Cal, who gave him a small thumbs-up.

"I'm impressed," she said finally, thumbing through the folder. "This is much more in-depth than I'd expected. You went to a lot of trouble here, and I appreciate it."

But…

"But you were right in the beginning. You're a small, family business. And this is a huge undertaking. I took this meeting because Miss Young insisted you were the best in town, and I can see she was right. But how can you three pull this off?"

The mention of Stella's name felt like a punch to Cal's stomach. He shifted uncomfortably in his chair, clearing his throat when Travis didn't respond.

"Ms. Ki— sorry, Caroline," he corrected when she tilted her head and furrowed her brow. "I started in this industry as a grunt on a job site. Travis was a window cleaner, and Jase was a glorified errand boy. We were teenagers who liked taking things apart to see how they worked. Since then, we've worked on hundreds of jobs, big and small. We can lay brick, install windows, paint a whole house in a day, and even do the landscaping if you ask. But we've also made a lot of friends. The crew we have now is just the tip of the iceberg, and I promise that once we get the green light, it'll double overnight. And we've already been to the bank."

Cal paused and looked at Jase.

"Right," Jase said quickly. "We're in the process of getting a loan to buy some new tools and machines. Our operation might be small now, but we're expanding."

Caroline had been listening intently for the better part of an hour, but suddenly, something caught her attention. She gestured towards the door, and before it fully opened, Cal caught the familiar scent of Stella's perfume. He didn't need to look back; the tension from Jase at his side was confirmation enough.

"Sorry, but I wanted Stella to join us. After all, she's why we're here."

"I feel bad I missed the pitch. Sorry, Trav."

Stella swept into the room, put a hand on Travis's arm as she passed by, and took the empty seat to Caroline's left. The pair smiled a greeting at each other as she laid down a copy of the plan.

Trav?

"I went over this last night. I assume you're as impressed as me?" she said to Caroline, a slight smirk on her face.

"You knew I would be." Caroline chuckled, turning her attention back to Cal. "Mr. Morrow was just explaining why his— forgive me, but small company should get the job."

Stella nodded and locked her eyes on his. She didn't smile or soften her face when she saw him. Instead, she looked cold and distant, like they were nothing more than client and contractor.

Thrown off, all Cal could think about was getting her alone. Finally seeing her in the flesh was all it took for him to see that he loved her. He didn't give a shit about Jase. He didn't care about what had happened. He just wanted her back in his life.

But now wasn't the time.

"Well, as I was saying," he started, stumbling over his words. "Our crew can be as big as we need. And Travis here has the home number of everyone in the business. Trust me, they prefer to work with guys like us. We know the job, so we don't push. We know what it takes to get a ton of bricks in place, and we know how long suppliers can take with specialized items. So we don't call to complain. We don't ask them to move up deadlines because we know how they're set. It's about mutual respect, and we have that all over the state."

"The budget doesn't include the co-working space. What's the number looking like for that?" Stella asked, turning to Travis.

"We can keep it mostly in line with the rest of the units, which means no extra lumber or tiling. But the cost will change when you start adding private offices, soundproof booths, conference rooms, and stuff like that. I estimate maybe another thirty-five thousand to do it right. But the revenue from something like that will make it worth your while pretty quickly."

Caroline leaned over and whispered something to Stella and the man beside her. Both nodded and then sat back, eyes on the papers in front of them.

But Cal couldn't focus.

Look at me, dammit.

"I must admit that I'm far more intrigued than I thought I would be, and that's saying something after Stella sang your praises."

Caroline stood and moved around the table. She extended her hand and waited for Travis to stand.

"I'm going to need a few days to consider, and we'll be in touch when I've made a decision."

Travis scrambled to his feet and shook her hand, thanking her a few too many times. Jase and Cal followed suit, then froze, unsure of what to do.

Before the awkwardness could grow, one of Caroline's assistants approached and guided them towards the exit. Ms. Kim was already back in her seat, deep in conversation with Stella. It looked...intense?

That's not about the proposal. Does the client know about us?

Out in the hall, Cal watched the pair talk in hushed tones, Caroline even putting a hand on Stella's arm at one point. Eventually, they each smiled, and Stella stood. She strode out of the room and up to Travis, pulling him into a quick hug.

"This is incredible. I'd bet my house she'll say yes."

Travis took her hands and squeezed. "I don't know. I mean—"

"Stella?" Caroline's assistant called from the door. "Sorry, but we need that file on Arizona."

Stella looked into the room and saw Caroline leaning over the table, speaking to the phone in the center.

"Gotta run." She smiled and turned without so much as a glance at Cal.

"Stell—" he tried.

"Not here, dude," Travis urged, a firm hand on his brother's shoulder.

It was too late anyway. She was gone.

thirty-seven

· · ·

CAL TOOK the long way back to the house and walked in to find Travis and Jase high-fiving the crew. The air was thick with excitement over the new project and its potential payday, and his brothers were as excited as he'd ever seen them.

Not wanting to bring them down with his foul mood, Cal discreetly slipped back out the front door and made his way around to the back of the house. Alone, he paced, cursing his own goddamn stupidity.

He'd never seen Stella look so cold. He'd seen her hurt after breaking up with Todd and angry over Marco, heartbroken over Jenny, and furious with the asshole that hurt her friend. But she'd always had a softness, a warmth he'd fallen in love with.

Not anymore. At least, not for him.

He'd seen it when she spoke to Travis and even when she greeted Jase. But the moment her eyes met his, her expression shifted. Her face hardened, her jaw set firmly, and her eyes narrowed slightly, as if she was only speaking with him out of professional courtesy.

Maybe seeing him had been the closure she needed. Maybe she came to show him, definitively, that she was over him.

For Cal, the effect was the opposite. Seeing her again, even this distant, colder version of her, only deepened his feelings.

He loved her. Head over heels, rip your heart out, kind of love.

And he did forgive her. Not only that, he finally understood she didn't need his forgiveness. She'd done nothing wrong other than hurt his fucking pride.

"Hey," a voice called, pulling him back to reality. "You're missing the celebration."

Cal did his best to not look like a miserable asshole. But his sour mood was hard to hide. "She might not say yes, you know? Isn't all that a little…"

Jase shrugged. "They know it's not for sure, but you heard Stella. And she knows what this client wants."

"When did you give her the proposal?" Cal asked, hating that he didn't know.

His brother shifted uncomfortably, scratching the back of his neck. "We had coffee a couple days ago—with Travis!" he added quickly, seeing the anger on his brother's face. "We brought her the proposal to see what she thought. She knows the client better than us, and she gave us some great ideas."

Even with his clarification, all Cal could think about was Jase and Stella having coffee. Laughing, talking, growing close.

Fuck!

"I figured you…"

"Yeah. No, you did the right thing. Let's just hope it works." Cal patted Jase on the shoulder and headed for the door.

"Wait." Jase grabbed his brother's arm and spun him back around. "Travis arranged it and said I should be there. And I—"

"It's fine, Jase. I get it. We're good."

Taking the hint, Jase raised his hands. "She asked about you," he added. "Wanted to know how you were doing."

Cal looked away.

Jase rolled his eyes. "Have you seriously not spoken to her at all?

Cal shook his head.

"You're a stubborn piece of shit, you know that? She's in love with you, and you're gonna lose her over something stupid. Just because you're too pig-headed to forgive her?"

He's right. I am a piece of shit.

By the time Cal went inside, the crew was back to work. Travis and Jase ignored him for the most part, no doubt frustrated at his attitude. He didn't mind, choosing to keep to himself with busy work downstairs—anything to avoid going up to the bathroom.

The day wore on, but most of the guys left early at Travis's insistence, including Travis himself. By 5 p.m., Cal was alone in Stella's house. He stood in the center of the living room and smiled, proud of how it looked.

She's gonna love this.

"Trav gone home?" Jase asked, coming down the stairs in a hurry.

"Yeah. Thought you had, too."

Jase waved his phone. "Forgot this."

"Right." Cal smiled and gestured to the kitchen. "I'm just gonna check the windows, then head home myself."

"Oh," Jase said, snapping his fingers. "This came for you, by the way." He pointed to a box in the corner, then left, closing the front door behind him.

Cal grabbed the box and looked for a company name or invoice, mentally reviewing his most recent purchases.

Nothing.

There was no company name on the side or indication of who'd sent it. Just his name and Stella's address on top.

Grabbing a small knife, Cal cut the seal and lifted the cardboard free. His eyes widened when he saw what was inside.

The slim black box was smooth and matte, with shiny inlays in gold that read: Dark Desires. His cock twitched as he removed the lid to reveal a very sexy bodysuit and matte black handcuffs with black satin trim inside for comfort.

Confused, he lifted the lid and found a note attached to the underside. The black envelope was sealed with wax. Inside, he found a handwritten note.

Happy birthday, baby.
- Stella

His birthday was a week away, but she must have ordered it when they were still together. And since she'd had it sent to the house, he could only assume she'd meant for him to get the sexy surprise and call her.

Then that's what I'll do.

Cal grabbed his phone and found her contact. But his thumb hovered over the screen for a second too long. The front door opened in a rush, and Jase walked back inside.

Cal scrambled to put his phone away and close the box. "What did you forget now?"

Jase didn't answer.

Cal turned, his smile dropping in a flash, when he saw the fresh cut on his brother's face—and the man behind him holding a gun.

"Take it easy, and this doesn't have to end in this asshole's brains on the wall."

"I thought they locked your ass up?" Cal asked, trying to keep his cool. "You know, something about beating on a defenseless woman half your size."

He smirked and jabbed the gun harder into Jase's back. "No record. Why would they keep me?"

"You're telling me they just let you out?" Cal asked, incredulous.

"What can I say? My lawyer did his magic, and they let me out on bail. *Overcrowding.* They needed the space for serious criminals. Not wrongly accused men."

"Wrongly accused?" Jase chimed in. "We caught you—"

"See, that's the problem. One you're gonna help me solve." He pushed Jase forward and grabbed a roll of duct tape. "Tape him to that chair," he ordered, tossing Cal the roll.

Slowly, Cal did as he was told. He kept his eyes on the gun as he loosely wrapped the tape around his brother's ankles and wrists. When the guy turned to grab another chair, Cal carefully ripped a small section of the tape under the arm of the chair. Jase caught the gesture and acknowledged it with a wide-eyed nod.

"Here," the guy tossed the chair over. "Tape your legs and your left hand. I can handle the rest."

Again, Cal complied, keeping up the facade of obedience.

As he passed back the tape, he couldn't help but ask, "You got a name? Or are we just supposed to call you Daddy?"

He laughed. "Funny. How about you call me Boss? Or Mr. Turner?"

"I don't think so." Cal tilted his head to Jase. "I think 'Dipshit' suits you better."

That he didn't find funny. Turner brought the butt of the gun down onto Jase's already bleeding cheek.

"You really are a coward, huh, Dipshit? First you beat on a helpless woman, and now you need to bring a gun to a fist fight?"

"This isn't a fist fight," Turner snarled. "It's a negotiation. You're gonna call that bitch boss of yours and have her bring her Jenny over. Tell her whatever she needs to hear, but I want them *both* here."

Cal scoffed. "Why would I do that?"

"Because if you don't, I'll shoot the two of you in the head. And then I'll hunt them down on my own."

Jase coughed and spat blood on the floor. "What do you want with the girls?"

"They both need to be put in their place. And Jenny needs to drop the charges."

Cal laughed. "That's not gonna happen, Dipshit."

"Oh no?"

"No way. We won't let her."

Jase cleared his throat. "And Stella's not just gonna drop everything and come over. *Especially* not with Jenny."

"You don't know that."

"I do, actually. She's working late tonight. New contract and she's under a deadline."

Cal shot his brother a look, unsure if it was true. Turner narrowed his eyes, clearly suspicious.

"You seem to know a lot about your pretty little client. She give you her schedule or something?"

"Well, we are sleeping together, so yeah. I know when she's working and when she'll be home."

What the fuck?

Turner chuckled. "Good job, bro. She's a fox. Even when she was kicking me in the ribs, I thought about bending her over—"

"Shut the fuck up," Jase barked. "We should've let her beat you to death. Or done it ourselves."

Turner's smirk vanished as he pressed the gun against Jase's temple. "Call her. Get her here, and then she can call Jenny."

He reached into his pocket and pulled out Jase's phone. He must have taken it while they were still outside.

How did he know about the house? How long was he out there?

Turner swiped and twisted the phone around to get Jase's face. The screen lit up, and he quickly found Stella's contact.

"I'm not calling her. I won't bring her here."

Turner hit Jase again, and Cal thrashed against the bonds, his frustration boiling over.

"Hey, Dipshit. How about you let one of us go, and we'll see who's the real man?"

Turner didn't even glance his way. "Call her. Now."

"No," Jase spat.

With an exasperated sigh, Turner pointed the gun at Cal's head and cocked it, loading a round into the chamber.

"I'm not asking again. And if you say a goddam thing," he warned Cal directly, "I'll blow your fucking head off."

Jase clenched his jaw as Turner hit the dial button. It rang on speaker four times before Stella's voicemail picked up.

"Make it believable."

Jase waited for the beep, then said, "Hey, baby. It's me. I'm, uh, at the house, and there's an issue with the guest bath. The pipe burst or something, I don't know. Fucking Cal told me he'd checked it, but there's water everywhere. Call me back, okay? Love you."

Love you?

"Aw, how sweet," Turner mocked. "That better be enough."

"Fuck you."

Turner shrugged and grabbed a third chair, setting it down in front of the bound brothers.

"I guess now we wait."

thirty-eight

. . .

OVER THE PAST FEW WEEKS, between Caroline's extensive real estate proposal and another new client, Stella found herself buried in work. Most of the time, she brought files home to be with Jenny. When she couldn't, she let Jenny know well in advance so she could either triple-lock the door or go to her parents for the night.

Stella felt guilty, but Jenny insisted it was fine. Lately, she'd even talked about moving out on her own again, which was scary but encouraging. It hadn't been easy, but the fear had subsided, and Jenny was almost back to her old self again.

As awful as it was, having Jenny around had been a quiet blessing. With her company and the avalanche of work, Stella hadn't had the time to obsess over Cal.

Ever since that night with Jase, she'd done everything in her power not to call him. She said she'd give him space, and she meant it. But she missed him every day. Even after weeks, she was nowhere near over him and didn't think she would be any time soon.

Over the first few days, Stella clung to the hope that Cal would call, that he would appear at her doorstep ready to forgive and forget. She checked her phone obsessively, each notification sending her heart racing.

But as days turned into weeks with no word from him, her hope dimmed to a resigned acceptance that it might truly be over.

He's obviously made his choice. And it's not me.

Travis appeared to be in the dark about what had happened and didn't press for details. But she and Jase had talked it through. She'd felt her cheeks warm with embarrassment when he pulled her aside, but then he made a dumb joke. They both laughed and eventually fell into an easy friendship.

And somehow, in the last few days, Stella noticed a significant shift in her mood. Her heart didn't ache as much, and she didn't dread visiting the house anymore.

But the day of the big meeting was rough. Caroline unknowingly scheduled it on the same day as the preliminary hearing in Jenny's case. The pair went together, hands held tight, hoping to hear the judge say there was enough evidence to go to trial.

He did. But after the arraignment, Aaron Turner was released pending the trial. The idiot was pleading "not guilty" to assault charges and, due to overcrowding, was released—with a warning to stay away from Jenny.

"It's fucking bullshit!" Stella hissed when they left the courtroom. It had been all she could do not to shout out when the judge made his ruling.

"How can they just let him out?" Jenny asked, her voice a shaky whisper.

"It's his first offense, and he can afford bail. But don't worry, he won't—"

"What? Come near her? You don't know that. You weren't there when—"

"Stells, please. I just wanna go home." Jenny dropped her head, sobbing quietly into a tissue.

Stella had half a mind to storm back into the courtroom, grab the judge by his robes, and scream in his face. But logic won out.

She drove Jenny to her parents' place, promising to be back as soon as the meeting was done.

"You don't have to do that," Jenny said when she was settled. "I'm good here. I promise."

Torn, Stella hugged her friend and eventually rushed to the office. Part of her secretly hoped Jenny would ask her to stay, giving her a reason to avoid the presentation. She knew Caroline would understand. And right before the elevator door slid open, she thought about leaving. Just pushing the button for the garage and heading home.

But this had been her idea. She'd put their names forward, so the least she could do was show up. And she'd grown close to Travis over the past few weeks. Their friendship was different from hers with Jase—more grounded. They'd started texting outside the group chat, mostly about the proposal, but it was strictly platonic. Travis had even asked her for advice about a new girl he was seeing.

I have to be there for him, she told herself, taking the first step into the hall. Caroline spotted her and waved her in.

No turning back now.

Holding her head high, she sauntered into the room. "I feel bad I missed the pitch. Sorry, Trav."

Determined not to look at Cal, she sat down and flipped open her copy of the proposal. "I went over this last night. I assume you're as impressed as me?" Stella turned to Caroline, thrilled to see she was smiling.

"You knew I would be. Mr. Morrow was just explaining why his—forgive me, but small company should get the job."

With a small nod, Stella finally turned her eyes his way. He looked unbelievably sexy in a suit. His hair was neat, and his stubble was perfectly trimmed. He was tanned, too, and she could see small cuts on his strong hands.

Her stomach clenched at the sight of him, but she kept her face neutral, desperate not to let it show. Cal looked a little taken aback but finally got on with it. She felt a wave of feelings as he spoke, and could hear in his voice how much he wanted this.

So, she threw them a soft ball. "The budget doesn't include the co-working space. What's the number looking like for that?"

Travis took the lead like she knew he would. "…maybe another thirty-five thousand to do it right. But the revenue from something like that will make it worth your while within a couple of years."

Caroline leaned close and whispered, "I like the idea of this office space. That's not something I'd thought about before. But I'm still not convinced on the numbers."

Stella nodded confidently. "I have some ideas."

Caroline pursed her lips and turned back to the table. "I must admit that I'm far more intrigued than I thought I would be, and that's saying something after Stella sang your praises."

She smiled and told them she would need time to review the plan. That meant Stella would review the plan and tell Caroline exactly how much it would cost and how much they could afford.

Something she'd already done.

While Caroline shook their hands, Stella discreetly checked her phone. She had a text from Jenny.

Can you call me?

Stella quickly texted back that she needed two minutes and lifted her eyes to Caroline.

Seeing the concern, she hustled back to her seat, her voice hushed. "Are you okay? How's your friend?"

"I'm not sure. She just texted asking me to call." Stella lifted her phone again—no reply from Jenny. "They let him out," she whispered, leaning closer so they wouldn't be overheard.

"You're kidding?" Caroline put a gentle hand on Stella's arm. "That poor girl. Go. Call her back, and let me know if you need anything."

When Stella looked up, she was relieved to see Travis, Jase, and Cal in the hallway, looking like a trio of male models in their snug suits. She smiled at Caroline and stood, walking out the door and straight to Travis, where she pulled him into a quick hug.

"This is incredible. I'd bet my house she'll say yes."

Travis started to respond, but Caroline's assistant called her back into the room. He squeezed her arm and winked a goodbye.

Stella returned to the conference room just long enough to find the right file, her phone already in hand. Then she stepped into the hall, making her way to her office with her finger hovering over Jenny's name on the screen.

She didn't press call—not yet. She just stood there, staring at the name, willing a reply to come through.

She'd held it together all morning for Jenny, then smiled through the meeting for Travis's sake. But now, alone in her office, the pressure cracked. Cal's scent still clung to her senses, warm and clean and completely him.

Her phone was silent. Jenny hadn't responded. And suddenly it all hit at once—the fear, the stress, the ache she'd buried under work.

The tears came fast. And they didn't stop. She sank into her chair, pulled her knees up, and let herself break—just for a little while.

thirty-nine

. . .

IT TOOK LONGER than she'd hoped to clear the tears. Stella
hid in her office with the blinds drawn, breathing deeply until her
mind stopped spinning.

Then she called Jenny.

"Jen? You okay?"

"Hey, sorry—I shouldn't have texted. I just—"

"You know you can call me whenever you need to. What's
going on? Do you want me to come over?"

"I don't know." Jenny sighed. "I just got this sudden, over-
whelming feeling of dread. Like... it hit me all at once. He's out
there, Stells. He could literally knock on the door anytime."

"Your parents are home, though, right?" Stella asked,
suddenly alert.

"They're here," Jenny said, her voice small, uncertain.

"But...?"

"I mean... what would they even do if Aaron showed up? He
might—" her voice cracked, "he might hurt them."

Stella clenched her fists, her stomach twisting. "You know Jase
and Trav meant it when they said they'd help."

About a week ago, the brothers had arranged a coffee meeting to go over the proposal and a few issues with the house. Stella had brought Jenny along—she hadn't wanted to leave her alone—and once the business talk was over, the conversation turned to the trial. Jenny shared the basics, and both men immediately offered backup.

"I've got an extra room if that'd make you feel safer," Jase had suggested earnestly. "You'd just have to come with me to the job site. But I know the boss," he added with a smile, "and I'm pretty sure she'd let you work from her almost-finished office."

Stella had felt her heart warm at the offer. They weren't just being polite—they meant it. But Jenny had brushed it off, convinced Turner would be locked up soon.

Maybe it was time to change her mind.

"Serioulsy Jen. Jase and Trav—"

"I can't rely on them for the rest of my life," Jenny mumbled.

Stella bit her lip. "I don't know, Jen. I saw the way Jase looked at you. I think he might have a crush."

Jenny laughed. "God, don't. After what you told me about him, I don't think I could handle it. Talk about a messy love triangle."

"Jen, you know—"

"That you're just friends. I know. Would still be weird, though, right?"

Stella agreed. "I guess."

The line went quiet for a beat. Then Jenny asked, "How was it? Seeing him?"

A lump rose in Stella's throat. "Fucking awful. Like, worse than I could've imagined."

"Shit, babe."

"Yeah. Shit."

Fresh tears burst from her eyes at the thought of Cal. But she held it together long enough to ensure Jenny was okay.

"I just needed to talk. I'm fine. Promise. Go back to work. I'll see you later, yeah?"

"I'll be there. And maybe I'll bring Jase. Just in case."

They both laughed and hung up.

Stella sat still for a moment, letting the quiet settle around her. Then she took a long breath, wiped her face, and straightened in her chair.

She wasn't okay. But she could fake it a little longer.

forty

. . .

STELLA FELT guilty for leaving Jenny alone. Guilty for missing Travis's pitch. And guilty for how often she thought about Cal when she should've been focused on her friend.

The one thing she'd finally decided *not* to feel guilty about, though, was Jase. She'd punished herself long enough.

Talking with Jase afterward had helped a little, but it was their coffee meeting with Travis and Jenny that really brought things into focus.

He'd pulled her aside while the others stepped outside and asked, "How you doin'?"

She shrugged. "Okay, I guess."

"He seriously hasn't called?"

She shook her head.

Seeing the lingering guilt on her face, he said, "Stella, did you know it was me or not?"

"No," she said honestly. "I really didn't."

"Then fuck him. If he can't get past an honest mistake, then fuck him. I'm serious. He doesn't deserve you."

Stella wasn't totally convinced, but his words lingered. For the first time, she felt certain she'd done nothing wrong. She was willing to apologize for hurting Cal, but she wasn't going to grovel for something she hadn't meant to do.

That same stubborn pride was part of why she hadn't called him, no matter how much she missed him.

Still, her mind wandered. Constantly.

She finished an email and looked up, surprised to see it was already dark outside. Rubbing her eyes, she stood and stretched, then peeked into the hallway.

"Hello?"

A few night owls were still at their desks. She knocked gently on her way to the break room, offering coffee. One by one, they smiled and refused, quickly packing up, surprised by the time. She assured them she'd be leaving soon, too.

Back in her office, she sipped her stale coffee and stared at the open file on her desk.

She needed a break. From work. From court prep.

From Cal.

Fucking Cal.

She'd only seen him twice since *that night*—once at the house, and earlier today at the meeting. She'd long since given up hope he'd call, but it still stung to know he was actively avoiding her.

Thank God for Travis and Jase.

She suspected Travis knew everything by now, but if he did, he kept it to himself. Jase, on the other hand, constantly made quiet jokes when no one else could hear. And despite everything, she laughed. She'd shove his arm and scold him, but walk away feeling a little lighter.

Jase would've been fun—*if* she hadn't been so consumed with Cal.

The way Jase touched her that night had been electric. And he was undeniably sexy.

But it was Cal she wanted.

Cal's hands in her hair, tugging and twisting.

Cal's mouth on her neck, teeth grazing skin.

Cal's fingers slipping under her panties, finding her heat.

Cal knew her—how to tease, when to push, when to pull back.

He read her body like a map.

And that cock...

Stella stirred.

The office was quiet. The blinds were drawn. She'd watched her coworkers leave.

Her heart thudded.

She dragged her hands up through her hair and down over her body, her palms grazing her breasts before resting in her lap. She closed her eyes and pictured him—Cal, walking into the office, dark eyes locked on hers, stalking toward her in silence.

He would move behind her, pull her chair back, and angle it just right so she had to look up at him.

He'd place his hands on her shoulders, squeezing the tension away, then let one hand drift downward, under her collar, over her breast. He'd pop her buttons open, slip his hand beneath her bra, warm fingers cupping her.

Stella sighed, biting her lip as her fingers slid between her thighs.

With one hand, she pinched a nipple, imagining his mouth. The way he licked and bit and sucked. Her other hand teased her panties aside, fingers brushing against slick warmth.

She moaned, pressing harder.

In her mind, Cal dropped to his knees. He pulled her to the edge of the chair, his mouth replacing her hand, tongue flicking in maddening circles just shy of her clit.

"Cal..." she whispered, breath hitching.

With her eyes squeezed shut, she sank her fingers inside, curling them as she rocked forward. Her hips twitched. Her mouth fell open. Her left hand tugged at her nipple again, harder this time. She rubbed and circled her clit until her whole body clenched.

And then—release. A sharp gasp, her back arching as she came hard and fast.

Her breath slowed. Her fingers stilled.

She opened her eyes to an empty room, and just like that, the fantasy was over. The ache was worse than before. And all too quickly, the high was gone.

forty-one

· · ·

SPENT AND STILL WANTING MORE, Stella grabbed a pack of wet wipes from her purse. She ran one quickly over her warm pussy, took another for her fingers, then tossed them both in the trash. Sliding her panties back into place, she sighed.

She'd thought about Cal's touch almost every day for the last few weeks. But as much as she fantasized, touching herself was never the same. Sure, she got off, but she always felt empty after. She missed how he filled her completely with his thick length, the way he brushed her hair from her face, and how he spanked her ass when he fucked her from behind.

Goddammit. I miss him.

Her eyes drifted to the clock on her desktop—then widened. She'd promised to be home early for Jenny.

Shit, shit, shit.

Stella rummaged in her bag, grabbed her phone, and jumped when it buzzed to life in her hands.

Jase?

Assuming it could wait, Stella let it ring out, then texted Jenny.

> Hungry? Want pizza?

I mean...I ate. But pizza sounds good.

Stella smiled, thrilled that her appetite was back to normal.

Your folks?

Sleeping.

Guilt stabbed her gut. She should've been there before they went to bed—just in case.

Before she could reply, her phone buzzed again, announcing a new voicemail. She knitted her brows and pursed her lips, choosing to collect her things and head to her car first. She wanted to be on the road before she listened to it and potentially had to call him back.

She turned the key and waited for her phone to sync. Then she put the car in gear and pulled out of the garage as she dialed voicemail.

Jase's voice filled the car. And she knew immediately—something was wrong.

> *Hey, baby. It's me. I'm, uh, at the house, and there's an issue with the guest bath. The pipe burst or something, I don't know. Fucking Cal told me he'd checked it, but there's water everywhere. Call me back, okay? Love you.*

Love you? What the fuck?

Stella slammed on the brakes and snatched up her phone. A few swipes later, she opened the security camera app Travis had just installed. It was new, but it gave her access to the whole house.

She'd turned off notifications while the crew was still coming and going, but the cameras were active. Stella entered the code and scanned the thumbnails. Nothing obvious—until she opened the living room feed.

She gasped, nearly dropping the phone.

Fumbling, she zoomed in, tears welling when she saw Jase and Cal tied to chairs. A third man sat across from them.

The image was small, but she could see he had a gun.

Oh my fucking god!

That's why Jase had said, *"I love you."* He knew it would sound strange. He wanted her to check.

Does Jase even know about the cameras? Of course, he does.

Stella couldn't think straight. Obviously, whoever had that gun had told Jase to call her. And he'd sounded pretty convincing in that message.

Looking back at the screen, she watched in silent horror as the man stood and brought the gun down on Cal's face.

Then he turned around, and her blood went cold.

Aaron fucking Turner.

Stella's fingers flew, minimizing the camera app and opening her phone's keypad.

He wants Jenny. He couldn't find her, so he found me instead.

Her thumb hovered over the call button. For one wild second, she imagined grabbing a gun of her own, storming into the house, and shooting the bastard square in the face.

Problem solved.

But that shit only works in the movies.

So she did the only thing she could.

She called the cops.

forty-two

. . .

CAL'S WRISTS were raw from struggling against the tape. He'd been subtly working them back and forth since the moment he sat down, but once Turner applied the final layer, they were too tight to break.

Beside him, Jase was bleeding and furious—but he was making better progress, thanks to the small tear Cal had made earlier.

But then what? Charge the gun-toting dipshit with one hand still taped to a chair?

Cal knew either one of them could take the moron in a fair fight. But with the gun in play, there was too much risk. One wrong move, and someone might not walk away.

And then there was Stella.

Cal let his eyes flick briefly to the small camera tucked in the corner of the room. He didn't dare linger. The last thing they needed was for Turner to notice and start shooting in a panic.

All he could do was hope Jase's message had been enough. That she'd notice something was off—that she'd hear the "*I love you*" and get suspicious enough to check the cameras.

Unless she's used to hearing it...

The thought had haunted him too many times. No matter how

often Jase denied it, Cal couldn't stop wondering if his brother had fallen for her. And since he'd all but shut Stella out, why wouldn't she move on?

Jesus Christ, stop.

He shoved the thought aside, furious with himself for even going there, with a gun aimed at his chest.

"What's taking so long?" Turner barked, shaking the phone in Jase's face. "I told you to be believable. She should be here by now."

Jase rolled his eyes. "And I told you she's working late. Sometimes she turns her phone off."

"You're just telling me this *now*?"

Turner drew back his arm, and Cal took the hit.

"Call her again."

Jase winced and obeyed, relief flashing across his face when it went to voicemail again.

"Hey, baby. Me again. I *really* need you to call me. The water's flooded the whole first floor. I, uh… need you to come meet the emergency plumber. He needs an owner's signature. Okay? Call me. Love you."

There it is again. "Love you."

Turner spun away, muttering. Cal used the moment to catch Jase's eye. Jase was already glaring. He mouthed *knife* and gave a barely perceptible nod toward his leg.

Cal dropped his gaze to Jase's pocket and saw it—the outline of his wallet, and tucked behind it, his favorite folding blade.

Shit. No. Not now.

Before Cal could shake his head, Turner whirled around, pacing with his hands in his hair.

"Call her office. Yeah. You're gonna call her office and talk to her. Get her here."

"I, uh… I don't think I have the number," Jase stammered. "I just use her cell."

Turner froze. "You don't have her office number? The woman you're fucking?"

"Jesus, we're not married."

"If you're lying to me, I swear to God—"

Cal tensed. And then headlights swept through the room.

Turner spun to the window, lifting the gun. "What car's she driving?"

Cal and Jase didn't look—they didn't have to. The carefree whistle floating through the window was enough.

Their eyes locked, wide with dread.

Travis.

Turner turned back, gun raised, eyes wild. "Not a fucking word."

Cal opened his mouth, but it was too late. The door opened. Travis strolled in, keys in hand and a smile on his face.

"You two bonding over late-night beers without—"

"Shut the fuck up," Turner snapped, shifting the gun toward Cal's head.

It took a second, but Travis read the room. His smile faded. His shoulders squared. Cal noticed his hand tighten around the keys.

"You're the dipshit we caught trying to beat on a defenseless woman, right?" Travis said. "So what? She turned you down, and now you break into her friend's house to show her how big your dick is?"

Cal almost smiled.

We really are brothers.

Turner chuckled—then his face went cold. The gun went up and fired.

Cal cried out.

Jase screamed.

Travis hit the floor.

"You motherfucker!"

"I'll rip your fucking throat out!"

Turner smirked and spat on Travis before turning the gun back to Jase.

"Call your girl at the office and get her here. Or he dies next."

"Fuck this guy, Jase," Cal growled. "Let him do it. It just adds to his sentence."

"Cal, don't be a—"

Jase's phone rang. Turner grinned. "Here she is now."

"Jase, I swear to God—"

Turner pressed the gun to Cal's head. "Another word, and you'll follow your brother to the grave."

He hit speaker.

Stella's voice filled the room.

"Hey, baby. Is everything okay?"

Jase cleared his throat. "Did you get my message?"

"I did. Sorry, I was working. You know how it gets. Anyway, I'm on my way. Is the plumber still there?"

She sounded calm. Normal.

"Yeah, babe. He's still here. He, uh, needs your signature on some stuff."

"Okay. I'll be there soon. Jase? How bad is it? Be honest."

Jase glanced at Turner, then at Travis on the floor.

"It's pretty fucking bad."

"Shit. Okay. I'll be there as soon as possible, okay? I love you."

"I love you, too."

Fuck, Stella. Don't come.

Turner ended the call and pulled the gun away from Cal's head.

"Good job. How long until she's here?"

Jase shrugged. "She's coming from the office, so... maybe thirty minutes."

Turner nodded and wandered back to the window, using the barrel to push the blinds aside.

But Cal wasn't looking at him anymore.

From the corner of his eye, he saw it.

Travis's hand. Twitching.

Stay down, Trav. Play fucking dead—and we might get out of this alive.

forty-three

. . .

"I'M DISPATCHING units to the location. Can you meet them there? They'll want to see that camera feed."

Stella scrambled for her keys. "Yes, of course."

The dispatcher's fingers tapped rapidly on a keyboard. "Okay. I see the house is in a cul-de-sac. Meet the cars around the corner, on Franklin Drive, okay?"

"Okay," Stella echoed, heart pounding.

"How long before you can be there?"

She turned the key, and the car rumbled to life. "Ten minutes."

She ended the call and took a deep breath, her hands trembling as she reopened the surveillance app. It made her sick to watch, but she was terrified something would happen if she looked away.

No, he's waiting for me. That's the whole point. Why else would he make Jase call?

Newly focused, Stella tossed the phone onto the passenger seat, shoved the car into gear, and squealed out of the garage. Tears blurred her vision, but she kept her eyes on the road, not noticing her phone buzzing beside her.

As promised, the cops met her one street over, out of sight from the house. If Turner looked out the window, he'd have no idea about the dozen patrol cars waiting in silence, their lights off and doors open. The street buzzed with hushed movement as officers secured the area.

Stella identified herself to the closest badge and was quickly ushered to the sergeant in charge.

"Miss Young? I'm Sergeant Rawlings. It's your house? Your crew?"

"Yes," she choked, lifting her phone. Her stomach dropped when she saw the lock screen. "Oh my god. Jase called again."

"One of the men inside? Did he leave a message?"

She nodded quickly, then put the phone on speaker and dialed her voicemail. Her heart clenched at the sound of his voice.

> Hey, baby. Me again. I really need you to call me.
> The water's flooded the whole first floor. I, uh...
> need you to come meet the emergency plumber.
> He needs an owner's signature. Okay? Call me.
> Love you.

The sergeant had her play it again, then asked to see the camera feed.

"This is live?"

Stella nodded and tapped the screen. "That guy attacked my friend. He was arrested. His name's Aaron Turner, and—oh my god, is that Travis?"

She snatched the phone from the sergeant, holding it so close her nose almost touched the screen.

The big man sighed. "A man entered just as we arrived. We couldn't stop him without giving up our position."

No, no, no!

Stella stared at the body on the floor and gasped. "Is he... I mean, is he—?"

"We heard a shot a few minutes ago. We're mobilizing now, but I need this," Rawlings said gently, taking the phone.

He turned away to confer with his team. The uniforms began

moving in quiet formation toward the end of the block. With one right turn, they'd be in view of the house.

Rawlings returned. "I need you to call your guy back. Obviously, Turner wants you there. If he thinks you're still coming, he might stay calm. Just ask what's going on and say you're on your way. Can you do that?"

He offered the phone. Stella took it with a nod, her hands shaking. She tipped her head back, drawing in ragged breaths.

They need me. Cal *needs me.*

She dialed. As it rang, she forced herself to smile—hoping it would help her sound calm.

"Hey baby," she managed. "Is everything okay?"

Jase coughed. "Did you get my message?"

"I did. Sorry... I was working," she said, steadying her voice. Her eyes flicked to Rawlings, who nodded and motioned for her to breathe. "You know how it gets. Anyway, I'm on my way. Is the plumber still there?"

"Yeah, babe. He's still here. He, uh... needs your signature on some stuff."

"Okay. I'll be there soon." The sergeant twirled his finger—*wrap it up.* But Stella couldn't help asking, "Jase? How bad is it? Be honest."

"It's pretty fucking bad."

"Shit. Okay. I'll be there as soon as possible. Okay? I love you."

Cal. I love you.

"I love you, too."

She ended the call and immediately reopened the surveillance app. Then she handed the phone to Rawlings and sank into a crouch, her breath shallow as the officers sprang into action.

Moments later, two sets of boots stopped beside her.

"Stay with Officer Markem," Rawlings said, gesturing to the young man beside him. "We can't have you near that house."

"What are you going to do?" Stella asked, her voice cracking.

Rawlings held up the phone. "We've got eyes inside now.

We're confident we can take him down without anyone else getting hurt."

Then he was gone.

Stella followed Officer Markem to a nearby car and sank into the back seat, feet on the ground, head between her knees.

Up ahead, armed officers moved as one, ducking low as they rounded the corner. Behind the car, a crowd of confused neighbors waited in the dark. Men, women, and children huddled together, trying to make sense of the chaos after being rushed from their homes.

But Stella couldn't think about them.

She turned her head, staring at the corner. Waiting. Straining her ears for anything—shouts, movement, a signal of what was happening.

Nothing. Just the low whispers of the frightened crowd behind her.

"What are they doing?" she asked eventually. "Why aren't they going inside?"

Officer Markem leaned over. "They're making sure the area's clear. No stragglers. No crossfire."

It felt like hours.

Then, in one brutal instant, the silence shattered.

Screams rang out. The crowd behind her cried in panic as a loud *pop* split the air.

A gunshot.

Then shouting. A lot of it.

forty-four

. . .

TEN EXCRUCIATING MINUTES dragged by as Cal watched Turner begin to unravel. He paced back and forth, muttering to himself while checking and rechecking the gun. Every so often, he glanced at Travis's lifeless body, visibly shaken by what he'd done.

When Turner leaned in for a closer look, Jase snapped, "Leave my fucking brother alone, asshole. Isn't killing him enough?"

"He did this to himself," Turner whispered, nudging Travis's leg with his foot. It flopped limply back to the floor.

"We're gonna kill you, you know," Cal growled, his voice low and steady. "You're not walking out of this house alive." His eyes locked on Turner's. "You hear me? You're fucking dead, you pathetic piece of shit. You're a loser. A limp-dick, woman-beating loser. I bet you can't even get hard without using your fists, huh?"

That did it. Turner's head snapped up, rage flaring in his eyes. *Come on, Dipshit. Take the bait.*

"You forget who's got the gun?" Turner hissed, striding over to Cal and waving the weapon in his face. "I don't need you. I never did. I've got her boy right here, and the bitch is on her way. She'll call Jenny as soon as she sees this." He grinned and wiggled the gun.

"And then what?" Jase cut in, drawing Turner's attention. "You gonna kill us all? I thought this was about clearing your name?"

Turner frowned, shaking his head. "I didn't do this. No, no, no…" His voice faded, and for the first time, Cal wondered if this was more than revenge.

He's completely unhinged.

"You did this. Yeah. I came here to talk, man to man, and you freaked out. I shot you in self-defense."

"You shot him?" Jase scoffed. "What about me? What about Stella and Jenny? That self-defense, too?"

"They deserve it," Turner muttered. "They're liars. You're liars. *She's* a liar. Flirting with me all night. Letting me buy her drinks. Rubbing up against me. What did she expect? And then she says she's 'tired.' I mean, what the fuck, right?"

Cal rolled his eyes. "Of course you're *that* guy. Big shock. A woman turns you down, and your answer is to beat her up? Real big dick energy, Dipshit."

"Like you've never thought about it!" Turner snapped. "They've got all the power." He jabbed a finger at the wall. "They lead us on, then what? Thanks for dinner, but no pussy tonight. It's bullshit."

"You're a total fucking idiot," Jase spat. "The worst kind of man. I doubt you've ever gotten a woman into bed—at least not without making it a nightmare for her."

Turner's face turned crimson. He raised the gun to Jase's face.

Cal spotted how close Jase was to freeing his arm.

Get his attention, dumbass.

"Even if they did deserve it, you're not getting away with this," Cal snapped. "One guy, sure. Maybe you spin some self-defense story. But you're going to kill *us, and* the girls? How's that gonna fly? We're tied up, unarmed."

Turner turned the gun toward Cal. "Maybe your dead brother lost it. Huh? How's that? Maybe he had a gun and went crazy. Maybe he's in love with your girl," he added, turning to Jase. "He walks in and sees the two of you fucking in the kitchen and can't take it anymore. Loses his shit."

"And what?" Cal growled. "He's already dead. You think the cops can't tell who fired the gun? Who died first?"

Turner looked back toward Travis.

Stay down, bro. Don't move.

"So then it's you," Turner shrugged. "*You* went crazy. *You* killed everyone."

"Really?" Cal said. "You think a jury's gonna buy that I murdered my brothers, my client, and her friend because I was *jealous*?"

"They'll believe what I tell them," Turner said, his voice steadying in the worst possible way. "There won't be proof. Maybe I wasn't even here. I'll wipe this place clean and leave your bodies to rot until someone stumbles on the mess in the mor—"

The sound of tape ripping silenced the room.

Turner and Cal both turned toward Jase, who now had one hand free and raised in the air.

Turner's eyes went wide. He lunged.

"Trav!" Cal shouted. "NOW!"

Travis exploded from the ground, lunging forward and grabbing Turner's ankle. Turner fell with a shout, his knee cracking on the floor. Travis crawled forward, tackling him as they crashed to the ground. The gun skidded across the floor.

Cal's heart leapt.

Before Travis could reach the weapon, Turner scrambled up and punched him in his injured shoulder. Travis howled in pain and staggered away.

Jase didn't hesitate. With one arm and one leg free, he threw himself onto the gun.

"Jase!" Cal yelled. "Shoot the fucker!"

But Jase wasn't ready. Cal scanned the floor. He spotted the pocketknife Jase had dropped.

Without thinking, he rocked the chair, forcing it to tip sideways. Pain exploded in his shoulder, but he didn't stop. Like a flopping fish, he squirmed toward the knife.

Behind him, chairs scraped, men grunted, flesh hit flesh.

Cal's fingers finally closed around the knife. He jammed the blade against the tape and began sawing frantically, until his wrists were slick with blood.

Then the gun went off.

Cal froze.

A groan echoed through the room, deep and ragged.

Cal looked up. Travis was on his feet, teeth bared, rage burning in his eyes.

Not Jase. Please, not Jase.

The tape snapped on his wrist. Cal flipped over, breath catching in his throat. He saw Jase sprawled on the floor, blood pooling beneath him. And Travis—*alive*—pummeling Turner beside him.

Then the front door burst open.

Cops swarmed in.

They tackled Travis first, dragging him away and cuffing him. Then they grabbed Turner.

But all Cal could see was Jase. And the whites of his eyes.

forty-five

. . .

AT THE SOUND of the shot, Stella's entire body seized. Sweat prickled her skin as she reached for her phone—only to remember she didn't have it.

Markem edged closer to the corner, head tilted toward the radio. Stella followed, barely breathing, until the static broke with voices.

All clear.
Two down.
Send in the paramedics.

She couldn't hear the rest, but those eight words were enough to send her flying.

She tore around the corner, past Markem, toward the house—now ablaze with light and flooded with movement. Her feet pounded the asphalt. A siren shrieked. She veered onto the grass just as the ambulance roared past her, its red lights washing over the blue-clad figures ahead.

The vehicle skidded to a halt. EMTs leapt out, hauling a gurney as they shouted through the crowd of officers.

Stella reached the driveway just behind them.

A second siren screamed in the distance.

"Hey!" Markem grabbed her arm before she hit the steps. "You can't just—"

"Cal!" she shouted, ignoring him. "Cal!"

Markem pulled her aside as the paramedics charged in.

"Let them do their jobs," he whispered, gently guiding her face toward his. "Breathe."

She shook, body pulsing with adrenaline, fear, and nausea. But Markem's steady gaze—calm, kind—helped ground her. He raised and lowered his hand, cueing her to inhale. She obeyed. It helped.

He led her onto the lawn. She wrapped her arms around herself and waited.

And waited.

And waited.

The minutes dragged. Stella shifted from foot to foot, gnawed her nails, and cried silently.

I can't just stand here.

Markem was deep in conversation with another officer when she made a break for the door. Stella sprinted to it and flung it open.

She meant to call out for Cal—but the words died in her throat.

Jase lay in a pool of blood, EMTs pounding on his chest and charging a defibrillator.

No. Please, God. No.

"Clear!"

She flinched as his body arched. A medic checked his neck for a pulse.

"Again."

"Ma'am, you need to step back."

"Clear!"

Please, Jase. Come on.

"Ma'am?"

"Stella?"

His voice was a dream—rough and warm—and it broke through the noise.

She was on her knees and didn't remember falling. The cops were staring at her, and judging by their faces, she'd screamed.

And Cal had heard her.

Strong arms wrapped around her, pulling her in. She clung to him, sobbing against his chest as he squeezed her like he'd never let go.

"Make a hole!" someone shouted.

Cal pulled back just in time to see Jase stretchered out, pale and still. Then came Travis, upright but bloodied, giving them a shaky thumbs-up.

Finally—Turner.

The cops dragged him out in cuffs, face swollen, lips cracked.

Stella saw red and lunged.

Cal was faster.

He slammed into Turner, dragging him to the ground. Officers went down with them.

"CAL!" Stella cried as someone shoved her back.

Three cops struggled to pull him off. She watched, stunned, as Cal leaned in—his hands locked around Turner's throat, eyes wild.

He whispered something.

A fourth officer grabbed him. They yanked him off and flipped him facedown, holding him there while Turner was hustled into a squad car.

"You good?" one officer asked.

Cal grunted and sat up. Stella collapsed into his lap. She wrapped her arms around his neck, locked her fingers together, and held on.

"Jesus Christ, Cal. Oh my god—I didn't know—I thought—I..."

"Shh," he whispered, taking her face in both hands. "It's okay. I'm okay."

She wanted to kiss him. To tell him she loved him. To beg him for forgiveness.

But the sirens screamed again.

And together, they watched both of Cal's brothers disappear into the night.

forty-six

. . .

THE NEXT HOUR passed in a blur. Cal gently helped Stella to her feet, guiding her to the steps where she could sit safely out of the way. He then went inside and gave the police a quick rundown of events, standing just close enough for her to hear snippets of what they'd all been through.

Thankfully, since they'd seen the camera feed, the officers agreed to let Cal go to the hospital with his brothers.

"We can take a formal statement later," Sergeant Rawlings said, his mouth a flat line. "You should get those looked at, anyway," he added, gesturing to Cal's bloody wrists.

The men shook hands, and the police left him alone. Stella sat still, her eyes on the man she loved. He had his back to her and his hands in his hair. They were stained with blood and visibly shaking.

When he turned to face her, his expression was unreadable. She'd never seen him so cold, so guarded.

"I have to get to the hospital," he said, his voice hollow.

Stella stood. "I'll drive."

He didn't argue, and they rode in silence, only speaking to ask the nurse behind the desk how to find Cal's brothers.

The man directed them to a waiting room down the hall.

"We'll either call or someone will come get you when there's news."

Cal nodded and led the way, choosing a corner chair near the dark window. Stella sat a few seats away, on edge but a hell of a lot calmer than before.

"I should call my folks," Cal murmured after a few minutes.

Stella gave him a small smile. "Maybe I'll go find some coffee."

She slipped out before he could respond, her footsteps echoing softly as she wandered the hospital halls. When she finally found a coffee machine, her heart sank. No purse, no phone.

Fuck. I have to call Jenny.

She'd left her bag in the car, but the cops still had her phone. She eyed a payphone nearby, but she didn't know Jenny's number by heart.

Frustrated, she returned to the waiting room, hoping to quietly grab her keys.

Through the window on the door, she spotted Cal on the phone. His face was crumpled with grief, tears streaking down his cheeks.

Not wanting to intrude, she waited outside until she heard him say goodbye. When she walked in, he didn't look up.

"Sorry," she whispered. "I left my purse in the car. Are you... what can I do?"

To her surprise, Cal stood and closed the distance in a few strides. He wrapped his arms around her, pulling her in so tight she could feel the imprint of his belt against her ribs. His hands gripped her like he was afraid to let go. She could feel his tears on her skin.

She clutched his shirt and held on just as tight, her own fresh tears streaming.

When Cal finally released his grip, Stella's heart skipped, terrified that he'd step away and leave her cold and empty.

Instead, he gently cupped her face in his hands and choked out her name.

"Stella, I'm so sorry. I was such a fucking asshole. I can't believe I—" He dropped his head but kept his hands on her cheeks. "I was a jackass. A stupid, jealous jackass who couldn't see past his own fucking ego. I love you, and I should never have walked away from you. I should never have let you walk out that door that night. I'm sorry. Jesus Christ, I'll spend the rest of my life being sorry for what I put you through."

A jolt shot through Stella's heart, freezing her in place.

He loves me.

Warmth bloomed inside her, but her stunned silence made him flinch. Mistaking her pause for rejection, Cal stepped back.

"I know I don't deserve another chance. I know I blew it. But if you can forgive me, I swear I'll do everything I can to show you how much I love you." He took her hand and pressed a palm to her cheek. "I've never been so crazy over a woman. Never felt this kind of pull. It's...overwhelming. My need to be with you. And I guess I just...I lost it. Seeing you and...I lost my cool because I thought there was no way you could love a guy like me."

Her heart cracked at the words.

A guy like him?

Stella's brow knitted in confusion, which, again, Cal read as a rejection.

"Cal—"

"No, it's okay. I get it," he said, sitting down, shoulders slumping. "I get it."

"A guy like you?" Stella echoed, her voice rising with emotion as she dropped to her knees in front of him. "I'm fucking crazy about you!"

He lifted his head, his eyes widening in shock.

"Cal, I love you. You've been in my head since before you ever touched me. And since that day, I've been *consumed* by you. By the way you smell and feel and taste. You're like...gravity. You pulled me in, and now I'm stuck. I'm yours, Cal. Even when I thought you hated me, I—"

Before she could finish, Cal crushed his mouth to hers, capturing her words with his tongue and stealing the breath from her lungs. Stella melted, her body igniting with a heat she'd fantasized about for weeks.

This moment, his lips on hers, was all she ever wanted.

His hand wove into her hair, pulling her closer as the kiss deepened, each furious and desperate for the other's touch.

Until Cal's phone buzzed on the table.

Their lips parted, leaving them both gasping for air. Cal pressed his forehead to hers, a low groan escaping him as the weight of the moment settled.

Reluctantly, he leaned over and answered the phone.

"Hey. Yeah, no news yet."

Stella rose slowly, legs trembling, heart still racing. A breathless grin tugged at her lips—until reality hit.

Jase.

Travis had been conscious when he left her house, but Jase...

Please, please, please.

Cal hung up and sighed, reaching for Stella's hand. "Sit with me."

She noticed the tremor in his touch as she sat down beside him.

"Cal, I... I'm so sorry," she whispered.

"Stella, you don't have to. I told you, I was a jackass and—"

"No." She shook her head and took a breath. "About...what happened. If you'd never taken over the house, you wouldn't have had to—"

"What?" Cal turned to her, his expression softening. "We wouldn't have had to help Jenny. Come on, babe. We're big boys. And...shit. What if it hadn't been us? What if you'd been in that house?" His grip tightened. "This wasn't your fault. This was all on him. That fucking psycho. Don't blame yourself. They wouldn't want you to."

Kissing him again, Stella sighed and placed her hands on his face. "What did your parents say?"

Cal exhaled deeply, his hand moving to rub his forehead. For the first time, Stella noticed the blood on his wrists and gasped.

"Oh my god, Cal. You need to have someone look at this."

He glanced down, as if noticing the cuts for the first time. "Right. I…uh…guess I forgot."

Stella rushed to find a nurse but chose to stay behind in case the doctor came with news of Jase. Cal was taken to a cubicle, where they cleaned his wounds and wrapped him up. He didn't need stitches and was back at her side within the hour.

He'd barely sat down when a young woman in scrubs hustled into the room.

"Mr. Morrow?"

"Yeah. Yes. That's me."

The woman nodded and offered a small smile. "Your brother's out of surgery, and he's on his way to recovery. The bullet went through his shoulder and, luckily, didn't do too much damage. He'll need a sling and some physical therapy, but he should make a full recovery."

Stella exhaled, squeezing Cal's arm. "Oh, thank god."

"Thank you," Cal said. "Can I see him?"

"Soon. Someone will let you know. And we'll update you on your other brother when we can. I wasn't in the room, so…"

"Can you at least tell me if he's going to make it?" Cal asked in a quiet voice.

"Umm," the tech hesitated, mumbling at the chart. "Travis Morrow is in recovery, and Jason Morrow is still in surgery. His wound was more extensive and—"

"But he's alive? And he's fucking strong." Cal stood and clapped his hands, excited energy filling his limbs.

"Yes, he's still fighting," she confirmed.

Cal didn't wait for her to leave before pulling Stella into a bear hug.

"He's alive."

Stella smiled against his cheek. "He's gonna be okay. Like you said." She pulled back and looked into his eyes. "He's fucking strong."

When a nurse finally gave them the nod, they walked hand in

hand to see Travis, who was totally out of it but looking better than Stella had expected.

They hovered by his bed for a while, each silently praying to whoever would listen that Travis would wake up and grin at them.

He didn't. But he was okay.

Eventually, Cal motioned toward the door, and they returned to the waiting room. One worry down.

Travis is fine.

Cal called his parents again to tell them about Jase, and then Stella asked if she could borrow his phone.

"You have Jenny's number, right? The cops still have my phone."

"You didn't find any coffee?" he asked, handing her the phone.

"Oh, yeah. There's a machine just through the doors, but I didn't have my purse."

He rummaged in his pocket. Coins jingled.

"I got it."

Stella smiled as she watched him go, then dialed Jenny, who answered after one ring.

"Cal? Oh my fucking god. What the fuck is go—"

"Jen, it's me! Calm down."

"Stella? What the fuck?"

Taking a deep breath, Stella gave her friend the highlights. She left out her near breakdown, the fact that Jase was fighting for his life, and her reunion with Cal.

She knew Turner was all that mattered.

"He's in custody right now, and there's no way he's getting bail. This is it, Jen. He's fucking toast."

"I'm coming to the hospital. Right now. I'll get coffee and food. I'll stop and get you clothes. Do the guys need clothes? I'll grab something. What floor are you on?"

Stella could already hear her grabbing keys.

"Jenny, you don't—"

"Stells. Don't. I'm coming. Now tell me where to go."

Cal returned with two coffees as Stella told Jenny how to find them. Then she hung up, took a cup, and leaned back, resting her head on the wall. Cal sat beside her, grabbed her hand, and held on.

Together, they waited for news.

forty-seven

. . .

JENNY ARRIVED at the hospital an hour later, her arms full of bags, clothes, and takeout. Trays of coffee filled both hands.

Cal rushed to help, and the moment her hands were free, she dropped what she was holding and flung her arms around his neck. Stella couldn't hear what she whispered, but she could guess.

An apology.

Cal pulled back and smiled. "This isn't your fault any more than it is Stella's." He turned her way and added, "Right?"

"Right." Stella rushed forward and pulled Jenny into a hug, her heart beaming when she felt Cal's hand on her back.

The three of them sat together, quietly picking at the food Jenny brought. They downed all the coffee and waited for news on Jase, each of them tense and exhausted.

But it was the cops who ultimately broke the tension.

Sergeant Rawlings entered the waiting room with two uniformed officers at his back. He apologized for intruding but insisted on taking their formal statements.

Stella wanted to argue, but Cal put his hand on her leg. "It's okay."

Jenny and Stella listened in stunned silence as Cal recounted the ordeal, sparing no detail, no matter how much it obviously hurt him to relive it.

Stella's story was much shorter, but Cal reached for her hand and squeezed when she told the police about seeing the camera feed.

When the statements were signed, and the police seemed happy, the Sergeant nodded to his colleagues and dismissed them from the room.

"Aaron Turner is claiming self-defense." His deep voice was calm and apologetic. "He's saying he went to the house at your brother's request and that he only acted when you two attacked him."

Jenny didn't care for the calm delivery. "That motherfucker! I'm going to—"

"Jen." Stella pulled her friend back and looked at the cop with desperate eyes. "That's not gonna fly, right? You saw the footage."

"It's unlikely," Rawlings admitted. "But we can't ever be sure. What I *can* say is that he won't be getting bail. He'll stay behind bars until his trial. And with my eyewitness testimony to the security footage, I don't see it going his way."

Stella slumped as some of the tension in her shoulders melted away.

They each thanked the man, then Cal took him to Travis's room. Stella and Jenny stayed behind, stunned into silence by the swirl of emotions—relief, fear, guilt.

After a long pause, Jenny exhaled. "They must hate me."

"You know they don't," Stella whispered. "They're bigger than that."

Jenny choked out a laugh. "There's being the bigger person, then there's almost getting killed. I mean...shit, Stells. They don't even know me. And yet they're in the hospital, and I'm—"

"You're *fucking traumatized!*" Stella snapped, standing abruptly and raking her hand through her hair. "Don't minimize what he put you through. And if you asked any one of those men who *they'd* rather have in those hospital beds, you'd be last on the list. Even Jase would say so."

At the mention of his name, Stella's heart lurched.

Come on, Jase.

"Cal seems to be holding strong," Jenny said softly, reading her friend's worry. "And you guys seem to be... okay?"

Under any other circumstances, Stella would have gushed about Cal. She would've grinned and giggled and told Jenny what he'd said.

He loves me.

But it didn't feel right.

She sighed. "We talked. We had a...moment, I guess. He told me he's sorry and he loves me. But—" she added when Jenny's face lit up, "I don't know if it was just the adrenaline or fear. I don't know if he meant it or if he was just in shock, you know?"

Jenny's face twisted from happy to confused. "Of course he loves you."

Stella shrugged. "I don't know. I believed him before, but then things calmed, and now I'm wondering if he just got caught up in the emotions. And I'm terrified of saying Jase's name in front of him in case he, I don't know, takes it the wrong way."

Jenny reached forward and squeezed Stella's hand. "Talk to him. When Jase wakes up, and we can all breathe again, ask him to breakfast or something. I guarantee he's gonna wrap you up and kiss you like there's no tomorrow."

Stella smiled, and the room fell quiet again. Until they watched two uniformed officers pass by the window.

"Do you think I could see Travis? I...I just want to see that he's okay," Jenny whispered.

Stella nodded and led the way. They waited in the hallway until Cal and the Sergeant stepped out of the room. Travis was upright and smiling.

Rawlings gave them one final nod before leaving, and the girls hustled into Travis's room.

Jenny practically threw herself on top of Trav, who grunted in pain but laughed it off when she reared back.

"I'm okay. Promise," he added with a wink to Stella. "But I wanna see Jase."

"He's out of surgery." Cal grinned before ducking into the hall to speak with the nurse.

A minute later, he reappeared with an orderly and a wheelchair.

"Oh, come on. It's just a shoulder," Travis whined. "My legs work fine."

Cal laughed and helped his brother up. The pair then went into the ICU to sit beside Jase, who wasn't out of the woods but was holding strong.

forty-eight

· · ·

"STELLA?" Cal put his hand on her arm, waking her from a dark dream. "You ready to get out of here?"

Blinking in the dim light, it took her a minute to remember where she was.

"Oh, uh. Yeah. Yes."

Stella stood and stretched, her back a mess after sleeping in the hard chairs of the waiting room all night.

"I told you, you should've gone home," Cal said, smirking as she groaned and twisted.

She ignored him and asked, "Anything?"

Cal shook his head. "Not yet. But my folks made it finally. They're in there now. Sorry, I tried to come out to get you sooner, but they're...not doing okay."

She waved him off. "Please. Don't worry about me. I just...wanted to be here. In case you needed me."

If they'd really made up, he would've moved in, pulled her close, and kissed her. But he didn't.

Instead, he asked, "Wanna get breakfast?"

She was dog-tired and wanted nothing more than to sleep for a week. But she needed to know if their reunion was real. Or if he'd just been overwhelmed and sought comfort in the closest warm body.

"I'd like that."

They drove to a local diner, where Cal parked near the door. He didn't take her hand or rest his on her lower back like he used to. She walked in feeling cold, the nerves churning her stomach into knots.

The waitress was quick with their coffees, leaving menus without so much as a "Mornin'." No doubt she'd worked the night shift and was just eager to get home to bed.

I know the feeling.

Stella cupped her mug and closed her eyes, trying to breathe some of the tension from her shoulders. Across the table, Cal mirrored her—mug in hand, head rolling to loosen his neck.

"We must look like shit," Stella said with a chuckle.

Cal gave a lopsided smile and touched the menu. Neither of them read much, and when the waitress returned, they both mindlessly ordered short stacks with bacon. She refilled their coffee and walked away, taking their only distraction with her.

Chewing at the inside of her cheek, Stella finally raised her eyes. Cal looked worn out. His dark eyes were sunken, and he had cuts and bruising scattered across his face. He'd taken off his jacket so his gauze-wrapped wrists were on full display.

Stella wondered what the waitress thought of them.

She probably doesn't give two shits. I doubt we're the weirdest pair she's ever seen.

"How's Trav holding up? I bet he's going crazy stuck in that bed." She lifted the coffee to her lips as an excuse not to make eye contact.

Cal shrugged. "He's a big boy. They'll probably let him leave later today. Not that he will." He checked his watch and blinked his eyes a few times to focus. "He'll just take up shop in Jase's room until he...uh, he wakes up."

Stella didn't know what to say, but the way Cal was checking his watch dimmed her hopes of a happy ending.

The food arrived within minutes, and Cal robotically shoveled the pancakes and bacon into his mouth. Stella was surprised to feel her stomach growl at the sight of it and eagerly devoured the first pancake in four big bites.

Cal finished the plate in record time, sitting back and stretching out so his stomach could digest more easily. Stella made it through more than half and gave up, knowing she'd never finish the whole thing.

Neither spoke a word, and they only made eye contact once during their meal. And the longer it went on, the more Stella assumed it was over between them.

When the waitress came for their plates, Stella asked for the check, and for the first time since they'd arrived, Cal looked up at her and smiled.

"You got somewhere to be?"

Confused, Stella shrugged. "I just figured…we're both tired, and you probably wanna get back to the hospital."

"Stella, I—"

"You want the check or not?" the waitress interrupted.

"Can we have another couple of coffees first? Maybe a few minutes to digest?"

The tired woman rolled her eyes and left them to it.

"Cal—"

"Please. Let me?"

Stella tensed and went quiet, unsure if she wanted to hear what came next.

Cal blew out a breath and ran a hand through his hair. Without really thinking about it, Stella glanced at his arm. It was more tanned now and seemed more toned, if that was possible.

"I guess I should apologize for what happened at the hospital. You—*we* were in shock, and I shouldn't have just jumped like that."

No, no, no.

Stella's heart sank into her gut.

"And I know that asking you to forgive me after all this time is kind of fucking bullshit, but...what have I got to lose, right? I mean, I should've called and—"

"Wait," Stella stammered. "I'm confused. You're apologizing for kissing me, but then asking *me* to forgive *you*?"

Isn't he the one who needs to forgive me?

Cal's fists clenched on the table. "I know. Shit. Why should you forgive me?"

Stella reached over and laid her hand on his. "Stop. Take a breath. We're not doing this right. And I don't want you walking out that door because of a stupid miscommunication."

He looked up, hope flickering in his eyes.

"Did you mean what you said at the hospital? Or are you apologizing because you didn't? Was it just the shock, and now it's worn off?"

Something clicked in Cal's head. "What? No—I mean, yes. I meant it. I'm apologizing because I...I was a dick. A self-righteous, selfish coward. And I blurted all that out without even thinking about whether or not you could forgive me."

He shook his head and dropped his eyes. "I should've asked you to stay that night. Or at least fucking called you the next day. I wanted to. I really did. I just..." His dark eyes reached her again. "I was scared."

"Scared? Scared of what?"

"This went from casual fucking to lo— something *more* really fast. And at first, I was totally okay with that. But when I saw you with Jase..."

Stella felt his hands tighten and saw his jawline harden.

"It almost broke me. I felt like you'd reached in and ripped my fucking heart out."

"Cal..."

"I know you didn't mean to, and I know Jase didn't either. I *know* that. The truth is, I forgave you both almost right away. It wasn't even about forgiving you. It was my shit. It was me seeing you with another guy and being fucking terrified that you'll realize you can do so much better than me. Whether that's Jase or someone else. And I guess I hated Jase for making me feel that way. For making me see how fucking insecure I am."

Stella sat with her mouth open, completely at a loss for words.

He's insecure?

She ran her thumb over his knuckles and took a deep breath, wanting to make every word as clear as possible.

"I thought you hated me. I thought you never wanted to see me again. But all this time…Cal, I don't know what to say other than…*fuck*. Everything I said to you last night was the truth. I have never felt like this about anyone. I've been killing myself for weeks thinking you thought I had feelings for Jase. And I need you to know that I don't. I never have, and I never will. He's a great guy, and yeah, obviously, he's attractive, but all I want is you. You're all I've thought about since you first walked into my house. Before I even knew your name, you were in my dreams. And now?" Stella laughed and shook her head.

It's now or never.

"I love you, Cal. I love your smile and your dark sense of humor. I love how passionate you are about your work and my house, and I love that you're so giving with your time. I love that you dropped everything to rush to Jenny's without me even asking, and I love how you protected her and made her feel safe. I love that you didn't push me to come see you when you knew I needed to be with her, but that you also made it clear you still wanted me."

She reached across the table and held his gaze. " I love the way you make me feel and the way your hands set my skin on fire. Cal, I fucking love you. Not Jase or Travis or some other hypothetical dude. There is nobody 'better for me' because you're it. My gravity. You make my life better, and I just want you to come back to me."

A slow, stunned smile spread across Cal's face. Stella could see the tension vanish from his shoulders. He braced himself on the table and stood, leaning over to kiss her.

"That's really sweet," the waitress said, snapping her gum. "You want the check now?"

forty-nine

. . .

CAL PAID the check and placed a hand on Stella's back, guiding her out to his truck with quick, urgent steps. She could feel the tension in his touch, but this time, it wasn't fear or guilt.

It was all lust.

He kept his eyes on the asphalt and flexed his grip on the steering wheel, pressing the gas a little too hard on the early morning roads. Not that Stella minded. She was pretty sure they were both thinking the same thing—the sooner they could get naked, the better.

He parked a block from her Airbnb, and they hustled up the sidewalk, through the front door of the building, and down the hall to her temporary apartment. His hand slid to her waist as she fumbled for her keys, his nose brushing her hair.

Stella cursed herself for not doing it in the truck. Her hands trembled as she shoved things around in her bag, all too aware of Cal behind her.

When his lips found her neck, she bit back a moan.

"Cal," she warned. "You need to let me find the keys, because this is not happening in the hallway."

"This is happening in the next thirty seconds, no matter where we are," he growled into her ear.

Her body tightened, heat rising to her collar. She frantically searched until her fingers finally grazed the fob. In seconds, the key was in the lock and turning. They stumbled inside, the door slamming behind them, keys forgotten on the outside.

Cal spun her around and kissed her so hard she could barely breathe. She tossed her bag to the floor and slid her hands into his hair, groaning as he explored her body like he couldn't get enough.

They knocked over a barstool as they backed into the couch. Cal caught her with one hand on her back and the other braced on the cushion, easing them down—but only for a second. Then he was back on her, hungry and insistent.

She'd missed this—the feel of his body above hers, the smirk she could feel on his lips, his hands slipping under her shirt, and the low moan he made when he found her breasts.

They pulled apart, panting, both flushed and buzzing.

"Should we slow down?" he asked, breathless and grinning.

It only made her love him more. She wanted this to last, but her body wasn't willing to wait. She'd been wet since he gave her that look in the diner, and all she wanted now was to feel him inside.

She tightened her grip on his neck and pulled him back in.

Her hand found him hard and ready. She eagerly worked at his belt, then yanked down his zipper, sighing when her palm met his cock through his briefs.

Cal groaned and reached to lift her shirt, wasting no time. He pushed her bra aside and wrapped his mouth around one nipple, then the other, rolling his tongue across her peaks until she gasped.

Her hand stroked his length, hips shifting as heat pulsed between her legs.

When he pinched her nipple a little too hard, a jolt went straight to her core.

"Pants off. Now," she ordered.

Cal stood and stripped fast, jeans kicked aside, shirt tossed.

Stella was already halfway undressed and down to her panties in seconds.

She sat back and watched him pull off his briefs, warmth pooling inside at the sight of him. She reached for his cock with hungry eyes, but he caught her hand before she could take him in her mouth.

"I won't last," he whispered, lifting her into his arms.

"Then take me to bed."

He nodded, cupped her ass, and hoisted her legs around his waist. She could feel him rubbing against her entrance, and her pulse jumped at the contact.

They collapsed onto the bed with less grace than intended, both laughing as they shoved pillows aside.

Stella climbed into his lap and kissed him hard, wrapping her legs around his waist and angling her hips. She felt the head of his cock at her entrance, thick and hard. Cal leaned back and thrust up into her, filling her in one deep stroke.

"Oh, Cal," she breathed, her body arching.

He moved with her, one hand gripping her hip, the other smacking her ass as they found a steady rhythm. The tension built fast, the tight coil in her belly threatening to snap.

She could tell he was close, too.

Their lips crashed again. Cal slowed and flipped her onto her back, kissing down her body until he found her clit with his tongue.

"Fuck, Cal. I'm so close."

"Let go," he murmured. "I wanna see you."

"No," she whispered, catching his chin. "I want you inside."

He didn't hesitate. Cal crawled up her body, positioned himself just right, and pushed inside. Inch by inch, he filled her, his eyes locked on hers as she melted beneath him.

He rolled his hips, adjusting his angle, and reached between them to rub her clit with skilled fingers.

She gasped, moaned, then cried out as the pressure inside tipped over.

Her orgasm hit hard, body shaking, legs trembling.

Cal didn't stop. He fucked her through it, pace increasing as he chased his own release.

Her walls fluttered around him just as he groaned and spilled into her, both of them lost in the moment, wrapped around each other.

Breathing hard, he collapsed on top of her. Stella locked her arms and legs around him and squeezed.

"Christ," she whispered. "I missed you."

fifty

. . .

two days later

"HEY, DO I LOOK OKAY?" Stella asked, smoothing the front of her black dress for the third time in five minutes.

Cal glanced over as he adjusted the collar of his suit. "You look gorgeous," he said softly, the corner of his mouth lifting in a tired smile.

Turning to face him, Stella fixed the knot in his tie and ran her hands over the strong line of his shoulders. She lingered a second longer than necessary, brushing away a non-existent piece of lint before pressing a kiss to his cheek. Then she slipped her hand into his, and they walked toward the car.

The ride was heavy with silence. No music, no idle conversation—just the steady hum of the road beneath them and the mutual weight of what waited ahead.

When they pulled into the courthouse parking lot, Stella froze.

"I don't think I can do it," she whispered, her hand trembling in her lap.

Cal reached across the center console and rested his palm gently on her thigh. "You have to," he said. "We both do. For Jenny. And for Jase."

She nodded, eyes forward, and swallowed the lump in her throat. Then she pushed open the door and followed him out, heels clicking softly against the pavement.

The courthouse buzzed with activity. Strangers brushed past, voices rose in every corner. Stella tightened her grip on Cal's hand —first to keep from getting separated, and then to steady herself. The building suddenly felt too loud, too bright, too crowded.

They found Jenny and Sergeant Rawlings waiting near courtroom three. Jenny looked surprisingly calm, her back straight, jaw tight.

"Hey," Jenny said as she hugged Stella tightly. "You okay?"

"Me? Are *you* okay? You didn't have to come."

"I'm not here for me," Jenny said simply, her voice low and steady.

When the courtroom doors opened, they filed in and took their seats behind the prosecution bench. Sarah Booker, the assistant district attorney, greeted Rawlings with a quick nod and offered a brief smile to the others before turning to prepare her notes.

Stella focused on her. On the woman who would speak for all of them. She refused to look toward the defense table, refused to give *him* even a flicker of acknowledgment.

But when the judge called Aaron Turner's name, something compelled her eyes.

There he was. Clean-cut. Pressed suit. Smug as hell.

He looked like he belonged at a fundraising gala, not behind a defense table. The smirk on his face made Stella's skin crawl. She knew exactly what he was doing—playing the system. Polished and white. Clean record. He was banking on sympathy.

But he didn't look smug for long.

The judge read the charges, and Stella felt a flicker of justice with every one: assault. Aggravated assault. Kidnapping. Attempted murder. And that was just the start. He still had another trial ahead for what he did to Jenny.

Turner stood there like it meant nothing, nodding politely as if he was being scolded for a parking ticket. When the judge finally asked for his plea, the room held its breath.

"Not guilty, Your Honor."

Stella's hand clenched so hard that Cal flinched. "Fucker," she hissed. He didn't let go—just squeezed back.

The judge didn't react. She just made a few notes,and moved on to bail. The defense attorney spouted off the usual arguments —Turner had ties to the community, no prior record, was not a flight risk.

But Booker wasn't having it.

She stood, heels firm on the tile, and reminded the court that Turner was already on bail when he broke into a home, held two men hostage, and shot them. That he was clearly a danger. That no amount of family support could counterbalance the *facts*.

The judge agreed.

"No bail. Defendant to remain in custody."

Turner barely reacted, but Stella felt something shift. It was small, but it was a win. The judge set the next court date for two weeks from today—a pre-trial readiness conference—and then dismissed the courtroom like it was any other Thursday.

Stella checked her watch.

Eight minutes.

Eight minutes to face the man who nearly destroyed her life. Who had nearly taken the lives of two others.

Turner was escorted out in cuffs, but not before he turned and locked eyes with her. There was no remorse—just a silent challenge.

Booker saw it too. She leaned toward them as he was led away. "He's not getting out. I can promise you that."

Cal pulled Stella closer, pressing a kiss to her temple. "You sure?" he asked Booker. "We have him on video. Why not just plead guilty?"

"Because no one ever does," she said. "They all think they can win. He's hoping for sympathy, or a deal, or just to waste our time. But this one? He's toast."

"I just want this over," Stella whispered.

Booker gave a small nod and gathered her files, then left without another word.

They sat there for a moment, stunned by the emotional whiplash.

Jenny stood first. "Come on. Let's get some garbage food and go see Travis. He texted me this morning. Wants a burger so big the nurses will yell at him."

Stella chuckled. "Yeah. Me too."

They split in the parking lot, Jenny heading off to grab food, while Cal walked Stella to his truck.

As she climbed in, she looked over. "Maybe we should bring Jase a milkshake?"

Cal's jaw twitched. "I guess they did take out that tube. And if he wakes up, he'll want something…"

"I'll text Jenny." Stella grabbed her phone and sent the text. Then she whispered, "He'll wake up today. I have a good feeling."

She reached over and squeezed Cal's hand.

He smiled at her. "Yeah. Maybe."

fifty-one

. . .

IT WAS QUIETER in the ICU than Stella expected. So quiet she was afraid to breathe too loudly. Machines beeped steadily, and soft footsteps echoed down the hallway, but otherwise, everything felt suspended in time. Like the world had paused—everyone waiting on Jase.

She sat in a stiff hospital chair, one hand resting on Cal's thigh, the other tightly wrapped in Jenny's. None of them had slept much since that night. Not really. Exhaustion sat heavy behind their eyes, but no one had spent more than a few hours away. Not while Jase lay still in that bed, hooked up to more wires than anyone cared to count.

Travis paced near the window, his burger long gone, a sling tucked neatly across his chest. He walked in slow, careful steps, but his eyes flicked constantly to his younger brother's bed. Despite his own injuries, he refused to leave. It was like he believed if he looked away, something might change—something might slip.

Cal didn't talk much when they sat with Jase. Instead, he leaned forward, elbows on his knees, hands laced together like he was deep in prayer. Every so often, Stella would squeeze his leg to remind him she was there. He always gave her a faint nod or a slight twitch of his fingers.

It wasn't much, but it was enough.

The first day was the worst. Between Stella, Jenny, and Cal's mom, the room was almost constantly filled with sobs.

Cal's parents were wrecked—both of them. And who could blame them? They had two sons in the hospital and a third bruised and bloodied. Stella hadn't heard Cal tell the story, but she could only assume he'd played it down.

Not that it helped. His father paced, just like Travis. His mother sat beside Jase, her hand on his arm, whispering to him in hushed tones and reading aloud from a battered paperback. She ignored everyone else in the room.

It took thirty-six hours to convince them, but Cal finally coaxed them into his truck. He took them to his place to rest, promising he'd call with any news.

They'd already called twice, asking when he was coming to get them.

Cal exhaled sharply. "I should go get them."

Travis checked his watch. "Think they slept?"

"Not even a little bit."

Stella turned her gaze to the bed again as Cal stood and patted his pockets, checking for his keys.

Jase looked so different like this. Not just pale, but small. The boyish light was gone from his usually casual, grinning face.

"Come on, man," Travis muttered, resuming his slow march. "Mom and Dad are already on edge. Cal and me won't hear the end of it if you…"

He stopped and cleared his throat. Then gently tapped Jase's shoulder.

"You can't let me be the good-looking brother now. *Wake the hell up!*"

It happened so fast, Stella almost thought she imagined it.

Jase's eyelids fluttered. His finger twitched.

She gasped and grabbed Cal's arm. "He moved!"

Cal was halfway out the door and almost stumbled back to the bed.

"Jase? *Jase?*"

Jase's fingers shifted against the blanket. Then his brow furrowed like he was confused or the light was too much.

Another blink. A swallow. A faint sound from his throat.

Cal reached the bed rail like it was the only thing holding him upright. "Jase, can you hear me?"

Jase blinked again. His lips parted. "Why are you two yelling at me?" he croaked.

Travis barked out a laugh that ended in a half-sob. "Jase? Jesus, Jase. Are you—"

"Will you two chill?" Jase rolled his neck and licked his lips. "You're ruining my high."

Stella stood, mouth open, then laughed. They all did.

"Fuck me," Cal said, breathless. "He's back."

Jenny rushed to the side of the bed and brushed the hair from his forehead, whispering something too soft to hear. Her eyes glistened, but the tears didn't fall. Not yet.

Stella darted to the door and called for a nurse. A young woman came quickly, scanned the monitors, and smiled. She murmured something about notifying the doctor and quietly slipped out to give them space.

Stella stood back, watching Cal, her heart in her throat. The smile on his face made her eyes sting.

"You scare us like that again, and I'll kick your ass," he said.

Jase gave a faint smile. "You couldn't kick my ass if you tried right now."

Cal leaned in and pressed his hand to Jase's cheek. "Wanna bet?"

Travis stepped up. "Let's hold off on ass-kicking until the idiot can stand."

"Pussy," Jase murmured, holding his hand out. Travis took it, squeezing hard.

Cal stepped back and returned to Stella's side, wrapping his arms around her waist so tight, she thought she might burst.

"You okay?" she whispered into his ear.

He pulled back and kissed her.

Then, before he could respond, Jase called out, "Can I smell burgers?"

fifty-two

· · ·

FOR THE FIRST time in weeks, Stella woke up to silence. No hammers. No boots stomping around on her stairs. Just stillness— and Cal, warm beside her, his arm draped across her waist. She didn't dare move. Instead, she stayed curled in the cocoon of quiet, nuzzling closer.

He breathed softly and pulled her in tighter.

"Do you hear that?" she whispered.

"Mmm?" he hummed sleepily.

"Nothing. No men. No machines. Just us."

Cal chuckled, voice low and rough. "Thank god for national holidays, huh?" He stretched out with a groan, his muscles crackling back to life.

"You were so late last night." She pouted, reaching behind her to run her fingers down his side. "I missed you."

"Two projects. One very demanding client," he teased.

Stella rolled her eyes. "I'm not your big, demanding client. I'm small time now."

"Hey, you're the money. Nothing gets going without your say-so."

He slid his hand under her arm, trailing up her side until his fingers brushed the underside of her breast.

"We can't do anything unless you give the order, ma'am."

"You're not wrong," she mused, twisting until they were nose to nose. Their lips met in a lazy kiss. "So you should probably get to work. Wouldn't want to displease the boss."

Cal shifted above her, one hand on the bed for balance, the other slipping beneath the hem of her shirt. Goosebumps spread across her belly as his touch climbed. He nudged a thigh between hers, then ducked down to her collarbone, pressing soft kisses across her skin.

His breath tickled her neck. "Permission to proceed?"

Stella arched into him. "Granted."

He grinned against her skin, his hand finding her breast, his thumb circling her nipple until it peaked. Stella sighed, threading her fingers through his hair. His thigh pressed between hers, nudging gently against her growing heat.

"I see what you're doing," she murmured, squeezing the back of his neck. "Tease."

"Not a tease if I follow through."

Without warning, he rolled her onto her stomach and straddled her legs.

"Oh no you don't—" she started, laughing, but he held her hips and kissed her spine, lifting her shirt as he went. When she raised her hips in protest, he smacked her gently. She gasped— part surprise, part pleasure.

"Still teasing?" he asked, fingers curling under the waistband of her panties.

"Only if you stop now."

With a groan, Cal shifted, one hand anchoring beside her while the other dipped beneath the fabric. His fingers found her wet and ready. He slipped one inside her slowly, then another, curling just enough to make her hips twitch.

She opened her legs further, and he moved between them, lowering his mouth to her center. His tongue was warm and confident, licking and teasing until she whimpered into the pillow. When he added pressure with his thumb, circling her clit just right, she gasped and bucked.

"Wait—" she managed, breath ragged. "I want you."

He didn't hesitate. Cal pulled her up, flipped her gently onto her back, and stripped off his clothes in seconds. She was already tugging off her panties when he returned to the bed.

Stella reached for him, taking his cock in her hand. She kissed the tip, swirling her tongue slowly. He groaned, one hand gripping her hair, the other bracing on the mattress.

"Jesus, Stella."

She took him deeper, her hand stroking what her mouth couldn't reach, until his hips twitched and he pulled her back.

"I need to be inside you," he growled, kissing her hard.

"Then do it."

He pushed her back on the bed and moved between her knees. Stella reached down and guided him in, both of them groaning as he slid inside—deep and thick and perfect.

They moved in rhythm, hips grinding, breath catching. His hand found her clit again, and she moaned his name, louder now. He thrust deeper, working her with slow, deliberate strokes until her whole body trembled.

She came hard, legs shaking, body arching as he continued to move through her climax. He was close too—she could tell by the way his grip tightened, his pace faltered.

Stella pulled him in tighter. "Cum with me."

A few more thrusts and he did, groaning her name into her neck, his body stiffening as he spilled inside her. They collapsed in a tangled heap, hearts racing.

He kissed her shoulder, then her jaw. "Fuck, I missed you."

Stella smiled, still breathless. "We should give the crew more days off."

fifty-three

· · ·

STELLA PADDED to the bathroom and turned on the water. Cal was in and out in minutes—a quick rinse of his spent cock, and he was good to go.

"I'll get the coffee started?"

With a small nod, Stella smiled and watched his tight ass saunter out. She closed her eyes and let her head fall back as the water warmed her skin. She kept her hair out of the stream but made sure to thoroughly wash away any trace of Cal's jizz. The last thing she wanted was to have a dribble left on her ankle when his folks arrived.

After a few too many indulgent minutes, she finally turned off the water. The last drops sank into the drain, and she took a moment to admire the room—her perfect, wonderful bathroom.

In truth, she'd been terrified to come back to the house. Terrified to invite Cal over. Terrified to imagine him in the room that had nearly broken them. She'd been sure he'd walk in and only ever picture her with Jase.

But to her surprise, he hadn't even hesitated.

They'd even christened the place the day it was officially finished—starting right there, by the window.

Now all that was left were the finishing touches. Some furniture. A few kitchen items. Photos and paintings for the walls. The crew still had some painting to do and one last epoxy floor to pour in the garage, but then they'd be done.

I'm going to miss those guys.

Living in the house with workers over the past month had been tough, but Stella had needed to reclaim her space from the tragedy. To take it back from the horror of almost losing Cal and his brothers.

Cal had made sure the floors were replaced, and every trace of Turner's presence was wiped away. Within a few days, walking in felt like it had never happened.

She chose a long dress that showed zero cleavage, wandered through her master suite, and headed downstairs. Cal was already cooking a breakfast feast, so she grabbed the coffee he'd poured and stepped out onto the deck.

The sun was shining, and her beautiful new outdoor kitchen was begging to be used. She'd decided to wait until Jase was home and well enough to join. It hadn't felt right grilling without him.

Today, they'd finally make it happen.

She had meat marinating in the fridge and plenty of beer ready. Cal's mom was bringing her famous mac and cheese. Jenny insisted on baking a cake.

All Stella could hope for was that the gathering would go smoothly. She'd met Cal's parents at the hospital and seen Jase a few times since—but this would be their first proper, normal moment together. It would either be incredibly awkward... or the official beginning of something new.

Please let it be the latter.

Soon enough, her cup was empty, and something delicious drifted from the kitchen.

The new table was covered in food—bagels, eggs, pancakes, and bacon.

"This is a lot of food," she laughed, topping off her mug. "We're not feeding the whole block."

"Have you seen my brothers eat?" Cal said, pouring his second cup and rinsing out the pot.

He'd just refilled the tank when the doorbell rang.

Stella hurried over, opening the door to find Travis, Jase, their parents, and Jenny.

"Hi, come in!"

She hugged them all one by one, but hesitated when Jase stepped inside. Then, trusting Cal's word that he'd made peace with it all, she wrapped her arms gently around Jase's waist.

She rested her head on his chest. "It's good to see you."

Jase had been out of it for nearly a week after the shooting and on bed rest for most of the month. Since he'd started walking again, they hadn't had a real moment alone.

Jase smirked, taking her hand. "I'm hard to get rid of. Ask my brother."

"Are you sure you want us here all day?" Travis asked, already leaning over the table to swipe a piece of bacon.

Stella lifted her arms with a shrug. "Booker said the judge will announce the sentencing around noon. I just thought… we should all be together. No matter what."

In the end, the food was *just* enough. Cal had been right—the boys inhaled half of it on their own.

"Got your appetite back, huh?" Cal said, slapping Jase on the shoulder.

"If I see another fucking smoothie, I'll throw it at the wall."

"Not these walls," Stella warned. "You know how much they cost."

She watched the two of them—Cal and Jase—laughing side by side. They looked completely at ease. And for the first time in a long time, she felt that way too.

Travis and Jenny insisted on doing the dishes while Cal and Stella gave his parents a tour of the house. Stella had, of course, offered them her guest room, but they were still staying with Jase —he needed the help, and it made more sense.

Still, both parents kept dropping hints about visiting again.

"You're always welcome," Stella said, winking at Cal.

When they reached the wardrobe and ensuite, she let the parents go in alone. Something about touring the room where she'd both *fucked* and *almost-fucked* two of their sons felt... gross.

She headed downstairs, passing a sleeping Jase on the couch, then rounded the corner and stopped short. Jenny and Travis were in the kitchen, arms around each other, grinning like idiots.

"Hi," she said, smirking.

Travis laughed. Jenny bit her lip and let Stella drag her into the guest room.

"You *bitch*! How could you not tell me?" Stella whispered, eyes wide and beaming.

Jenny squealed. "I know. I'm sorry! We just... didn't want to say anything. Not until we knew everything was okay."

Stella gaped. "When did it start?"

Jenny bit her lip again. "Not long after... you know. He texted me to ask how I was. Then I called. And we kept texting and calling, and... he came by with coffee and snacks. He's so goddamn sweet, Stells."

Stella pulled her into a hug with a happy shriek. "I'm so fucking happy for you. Travis is amazing. He's—"

"The only one you didn't fuck?"

"Oh, you bitch!"

They laughed and hugged again, the weight of the last few months finally lifting.

Then a phone rang. Jenny pulled it from her back pocket and swallowed.

"It's Booker."

Travis appeared at the door, raising a brow. Stella nodded, and the two waited as Jenny answered.

"Hello? Uh-huh. Okay. And what—right. Okay. That's great. Thank you so much, Miss Booker."

"Well?" Stella cried, grabbing her arm. "What happened?"

Jenny grinned. "Twenty *fucking* years. Fifteen minimum."

Travis whooped and spun her in the air, kissing her the same way Cal kissed Stella.

Fifteen years didn't feel like enough—not for nearly killing three men. But it was a win.

"Cal!" Stella shouted. "Get the champagne!"

She heard the thunder of his feet on the stairs and braced herself. Sure enough, he barreled in and swept her off the floor. He froze mid-spin when he saw Travis and Jenny.

"When the *fuck* did that happen?"

Stella grinned, took his chin in her hands, and turned his face to hers. "No clue. But I think it's great."

Cal laughed and reached over to clap Travis on the back. "So this is who's had you so chipper?"

"Chipper?" Jenny teased, nudging Travis with a kiss.

"Oh yeah. He practically skips onto the site."

"You're one to talk," Travis said, rolling his eyes.

Stella tugged Cal out of the room to give them privacy.

"You okay?" she asked, her eyes flicking to Jase still napping on the couch.

Cal followed her gaze and nodded. "Yeah. I'm good. We're good. *That's* good," he added, jerking a thumb toward the other room. "I guess now we just gotta find someone for Jase."

Stella smirked. "Funny you should say that. I kind of think one of the interns has a thing for him. The blonde who keeps volunteering to come with me to the site?"

Cal ran a hand through her hair. "And here I thought he liked brunettes."

Stella gaped. "Did you just make a joke about—"

"I guess I did. See? I've grown. And all it took was a couple of bullets."

"You didn't even get shot!" she laughed, wrapping her arms around his neck. "Thank god."

He nudged her nose with his. "I love you."

She kissed him hard, tongue slipping past his grin.

"Are you four done yet?" Jase called from the couch. "Because I'm *starving*."

Stella chuckled and untangled herself from Cal. "You ready to test the grill?" she asked, eyes twinkling.

"Yeah," Jase groaned, pushing to his feet. "And I'll take that blonde's number, too."

thank you for reading

If you enjoyed the story, I hope you'll consider leaving a review!

Continue to the next page to find out about my other romance novel, Three Nights In Stockholm.

also by elizabeth hardy

Three Nights In Stockholm

As a pilot, Remi flies all over the world. She's been everywhere you can think of and met plenty of men along the way.

In Paris, there's Sebastien, a sexy bar manager with a thing for kink.

In Tallinn, she's got Risto, a big, beautiful Chef she can't keep her hands off.

Her life is perfect. She loves her job, and her collection of lovers keeps her plenty busy.

That is until she meets Mats. It's lust at first sight, and it's not long before she winds up in his bed.

They have what was supposed to be one incredible night together.

And then the storm hit.

Now she's stuck in Stockholm with a man she can't get enough of. But is he what she really wants?

Printed in Dunstable, United Kingdom